BEARLY EVIDENT

To Danielle
Enjoy the Book!

Joes Schmelt

The Kristy Farrell Mysteries by Lois Schmitt:

Monkey Business

Something Fishy

Playing Possum

Bearly Evident

BEARLY EVIDENT

A Kristy Farrell Mystery

LOIS SCHMITT

Encircle Publications
Farmington, Maine, U.S.A.

Editor: Cynthia Brackett-Vincent

Book design by Deirdre Wait

Cover design by Christopher Wait
Cover images © Getty Images

Published by:

Encircle Publications
PO Box 187
Farmington, ME 04938

info@encirclepub.com
http://encirclepub.com

To My Grandchildren

Logan & Emma

Always in my Heart

CHAPTER 1

The sudden roar made me jump.

"That was Bella," Nick Lamonica said, pointing to a brown bear who was lumbering from his cave toward a pond. Nick was the head animal keeper for the Happy Place Animal Sanctuary.

I'm Kristy Farrell, former English teacher turned reporter for *Animal Advocate Magazine*. I was writing a story on the sanctuary and the many animals it rescued. Bella was the most recent inhabitant—she arrived four days ago.

The bear entered the pond, causing a huge splash. Only her head remained above the water as she appeared to survey her surroundings.

"Bella spent her entire life in a circus," Nick said. "She lived in a fifteen by fifteen foot cage and was only let out for training and when she was performing. Now she finally has space to roam. She has trees, a cave, and a pond."

The bear looked as if it were grinning. Can a bear grin?

"C'mon," Nick continued. "I want to show you the wolves."

As we strolled down the tree shaded path, I gave Nick a quick once-over. He was built like a fireplug. I could easily imagine this short but muscular man hauling cartons of food and supplies.

"This is our wolf habitat," Nick said, pointing to a grassy enclosure in the distance. "Three acres divided into two pods.

Wolves are pack animals, but you can't add strange wolves to an established pack. That's why we have two separate areas."

Nick paused. "The wolves on the right are sisters who came from a roadside zoo. The pod to the left is home to a family of wolves raised as pets—"

"Pets?"

"We have more than a dozen animals here that are former pets. Monkeys, a wallaby, a pair of capybara, a crocodile, and a few wolves. You'd be surprised at the number of people who think it's cool to own a wild animal."

He shook his head. "These animals may be adorable when they're babies, but once they grow up, they're impossible to handle. That's when they're abandoned. The man who owned these wolves sent them here when a playful bite broke his finger. Wolves have powerful jaws—even when playing."

"Nick," a voice yelled.

I spun around as a woman approached. She was tiny and rail thin. Her short black hair provided a stark contrast to her fair skin, and something in the way she stared at Nick with her glacier blue eyes sent a shiver up my spine.

"The barn hasn't been repainted yet," she said, accusingly.

"You asked me two days ago. I'll get to it, but I have more immediate chores."

"You need to get better organized." She frowned.

"It will get done next week." He frowned.

"I also spoke to you about changing the food for the capybaras."

"I put in the order. The new food should arrive in a few days. In the meantime, our veterinarian says our current food is perfectly fine."

"He's an idiot too." Still scowling, she stomped off. "This place is a hotbed of incompetency."

Nick cursed under his breath.

"Who was that?" I asked.

"Maureen McDermott, one of our animal keepers. She handles our marine mammals, monkeys, capybaras, wallabies, and other small creatures."

He shrugged. "Like most sanctuaries, we don't have the funds to do all we want. More staff would be great. Sometimes things like repainting a barn are not our top priority. But we take excellent care of our animals."

"She seems impatient," I said.

Silence.

"Off the record," I said. Although I couldn't print what he told me, off the record remarks often helped me form a picture of what was happening.

He hesitated, finally nodded, and spoke up, "She's good with the animals, which is what really counts. But her people skills are terrible. She's demanding and short tempered."

Nick inhaled deeply. "She's also what I called back in school a *tattletale*. She goes to the director and reports every mistake her colleagues make."

"What types of mistakes?" I asked.

"I can't recall specifics right now. Minor things."

He narrowed his eyes and pursed his lips. I wondered if these mistakes were minor. But though we were off the record, I could tell he had said all he wanted—at this point.

Maybe "Happy Place" was the wrong name for this sanctuary.

CHAPTER 2

After touring more of the sanctuary, Nick and I said good-bye in front of the cedar shingled administration building where I had an appointment with the sanctuary director.

When I stepped inside the building, no one was sitting behind the reception desk. I spied two rooms in the back, adjacent to each other. Suddenly, the door to the first office swung open and a woman, whose age I judged to be in the mid-thirties, emerged.

"I thought I heard someone out here," she said as she made her way toward me. Her dark, curly hair reminded me of a French poodle. "I'm Gina Garone, the director. You must be Kristy Farrell, the writer from *Animal Advocate*."

As she extended her arm for a handshake, I couldn't help notice her diamond tennis bracelet and other expensive looking bling—diamond pendant with matching earrings and a rock on her left hand rivaling the size of a small planet.

I like to know something about the people I interview, so I had researched Gina. She was *new money*. Her husband made multi-millions with his construction company. Gina had spent her time volunteering for environmental organizations and animal causes.

When the Long Island Animal Rescue Coalition came up with the idea to create a sanctuary, Gina spearheaded the fundraising efforts, and her husband was the first to donate a substantial amount of money to purchase the land.

Cut to the chase—a board of trustees was formed and Gina named director.

"Our receptionist is on vacation this week," Gina said "Why don't we go to my office to talk?"

As we headed back, the door to the office adjacent to Gina's swung open and two men emerged. One was a tall, athletic looking Black man. I recognized him immediately and smiled. "Declan Carr. How are you?"

"I'm fine," Declan replied. But he didn't look fine. He smiled at me weakly, and frown lines creased his forehead.

"I see you know our veterinarian." Gina said, appearing surprised.

"Declan is a good friend of my daughter Abby. Declan and Abby were classmates at veterinary school, and they still keep in contact."

"Declan," Gina called sharply as he started to walk away. "Don't forget. I've set up a meeting for three o'clock tomorrow. Make sure you're here."

He turned toward Gina and nodded. "I will. And I swear, I'm telling the truth."

Gina sighed. "I don't know how we'll get to the bottom of this issue, but we will."

Declan swung around and now faced me. "I'd love to catch up with you, but I've got to run. I'm headed into Manhattan for the Veterinary Association's annual dinner."

"You'll probably see Abby there," I called as he rushed out of the building. It seemed as if he wanted to avoid me.

Before I could ask about the '*issue*' with Declan, Gina introduced me to the man standing next to her, whose thin face, pale skin, and thick rimmed glasses enhanced a scholarly look. He was probably in his mid-twenties. "This is Lee Adler, our business manager. That's his office next to mine."

Lee nodded toward me and then said to Gina, "I have the report you wanted." Lee thrust a paper into her hand.

Gina glanced at the paper. Her face clouded.

"We need to talk," she said.

"I'll be back in an hour." He headed for the front door while Gina continued staring at the paper.

"Is something wrong?" I asked.

"No. Just some statistics. Let's go into my office."

Gina's office was not what I expected to find in a not-for-profit organization's headquarters. The room featured an antique French provincial desk, two silk upholstered chairs, and a Persian rug. Museum quality artwork hung on the walls.

Gina must have seen the surprised look on my face because she smiled. "My husband furnished this room as a gift. Not a penny came from sanctuary funds. I like to be surrounded by beautiful things."

Gina motioned me toward one of the chairs. She sat behind her desk and handed me a brochure.

"This pamphlet contains a list of the animals currently living here, and it gives the history of more than a dozen of these poor creatures and tells of their lives before they arrived at the sanctuary. Most came from abusive settings in captivity. Others suffered permanent injury in the wild and can no longer survive on their own."

I stuffed the material in my tote bag for later and then asked her a series of questions about managing the sanctuary. Gina provided a great overview of the facility's operation, but she wasn't good with specifics. I think she realized she didn't have the information I needed.

"My main job as director is to bring in the money to keep this place going," she explained. "The actual day to day operation, especially the budgeting, is done by Lee. He's a whiz with numbers."

She grabbed her phone. "Why don't I set up an appointment for you to speak with him about the nuts and bolts?"

She called Lee and then asked me, "Can you be here early tomorrow, Kristy? Our staff is here by seven, so if you could meet with Lee at seven-fifteen that would be perfect."

I agreed, and we went back to the interview.

"Fundraising often involves getting donations other than money," she said. "For example, a local food chain donates a good portion of meat for the carnivores. And there are several other organizations that give us fish and produce."

"That's great. How much?"

Gina waved her hand dismissively. "I don't remember the exact amount. But Lee will have all the figures."

She leaned forward in her chair, rested her arms on her desk, and formed a steeple with her fingers. "We still need to buy plenty, but this does cut a hefty amount off our food costs."

Before I could ask another question, Maureen McDermott burst into the room.

"Not now. I'm with someone," Gina said, her voice rising slightly.

Maureen ignored the comment. "Did you make your decision yet?"

"No. I'm still gathering facts."

"I told you exactly what happened. Do you think I'm lying?"

Gina raised her voice. "I think you need to leave. I'm in the midst of an interview. I'll see you tomorrow at three."

I remembered three o'clock was the time she was meeting with Declan.

Maureen glared at Gina. If looks would kill, the director would be dead. Maureen said nothing else. She marched out of the room.

"What's that about?" I asked.

"It's a personal issue. Now, let's get back to the interview. I want to tell you about our next fundraising event."

Gina's voice was shaky as she continued talking. Was her argument with Maureen really personal, or did it have to do with the sanctuary?

What was going on with Declan?

What was on the paper from Lee that upset Gina?

But most important in my mind was Nick's comment calling Maureen a tattletale. Was she a whistleblower?

I was a reporter. Gina had to realize I wouldn't drop this until I found the answers.

CHAPTER 3

The next morning, as I poured my second mug of coffee, I heard a car screech into my driveway. It was not yet six-thirty.

At that time, it could only be one person. I grabbed another mug and placed it on the counter next to the coffee machine.

My two dogs, Archie, a large black dog of uncertain heritage who resembled a small bear, and Brandy, an eight-year-old collie, bolted out from under the table. Archie bumped his head, lost his footing, and slid across the floor. As he turned his head in my direction with a goofy grin on his face, he scrambled to his feet and joined Brandy by the kitchen door.

"Hi Mom." My twenty-seven-year-old daughter paraded into the house. With her dark hair, olive skin, almond eyes, and aquiline nose, she looked like a younger and thinner version of me. Our genes were definitely from the Greek half of my family.

Abby had joined her father's veterinary practice. She rented a nearby beach house with her fiancé, Jason, but she frequently stopped here for a quick cup of coffee since our home was only a few blocks away from the veterinary office.

"You just missed Dad," I said. "He left about five minutes ago to get an early jump on what he described as mounds and mounds of paperwork."

Abby nodded and grinned. "I know. He was complaining

about that yesterday. Ooh, I smell bagels."

"In the bag on the counter," I said. "Dad picked them up before he left. They're still warm."

"You've got cream cheese, right?" She swung open the refrigerator door and stuck her head inside. So did Archie and Brandy.

"I need to leave in a few minutes, so you'll have to clean up," I said as she smeared cream cheese on her bagel. "I have an early interview at the animal sanctuary."

"How did it go there yesterday?" she asked as she poured coffee into her mug and slid into the chair across from me. The dogs rested at her feet, hoping for crumbs. Dogs are such optimists.

"The sanctuary is great, but there appears to be a lot of tension. Most centers around one of the animal keepers. By the way, I ran into your friend Declan there. I think something was bothering him."

"Something is. I talked to him last night at the Veterinary Association dinner. He told me he lost a monkey on the operating table last week."

I frowned. "That's sad, but operations aren't always successful."

"It was a routine operation."

"But even routine operations can go bad."

Abby stared downward, appearing to focus on her bagel.

"Abby?"

"He was accused of being drunk when he operated."

I almost spilled my coffee. "That can't be true, can it?"

"Declan swears he had absolutely nothing to drink, and I believe him. But the animal keeper in charge of the monkeys was assisting in the operating room. She claims he was intoxicated, and she reported it to the sanctuary director."

"Animal keeper in charge of the monkeys? Is that Maureen

McDermott?"

Abby nodded.

"But why would she make an untrue accusation?"

"Declan doesn't know why she's lying. He claims she had it in for him from the day she started working at the sanctuary."

"Did he know her before he began there?"

"No. He has no idea what's causing her animosity."

From what I'd seen yesterday, Maureen McDermott appeared to have a chip on her shoulder. Declan wasn't the only member of the staff she seemed to dislike.

"Was anyone else in the operating room?" I asked.

Abby shook her head.

"Did anyone see him right before the surgery? Someone who can verify he was sober."

"He was home alone until he came in for the operation."

"So it's a '*he said, she said*' situation."

"Well, unfortunately, there's more. Declan had a drinking problem in college. He was a linebacker on his college football team. One night, after a winning game, he got drunk and narrowly avoided a car accident. That brought him to his senses. He put himself into rehab, and he hasn't had a drink since then."

Abby sipped her coffee and continued. "By the time I met him in veterinary school, he was done with alcohol."

I thought about all the times Declan had been to our house. I hadn't a clue he had a problem. "How come you never told me?"

"I didn't find out until last night. I don't think any of our friends knew either. When we were together he always drank water or soda. I just thought he didn't like the taste of liquor." Abby shrugged. "He confided in me about his drinking problem at the dinner. He's worried about Maureen's accusation."

"So, what's going to happen?"

"I don't know. But because he had a drinking issue in the past, it gives more credence to the accusation." Abby twirled her hair with her fingers. She always did this when she was nervous. "If the director decides against Declan—"

"Declan could lose his job." I completed the thought.

"And his veterinarian license." Abby shook her head. "That means his career is over."

CHAPTER 4

I left Abby to clean up as I scooted out of my house and drove to the Happy Place Animal Sanctuary. After showing my press pass to the guard at the gate. I pulled into the parking lot and made my way up the path to the administration building.

I arrived ten minutes early for my seven-fifteen appointment. The door to the director's office was wide open, and Gina Garone was sitting behind her desk. The door to Lee Adler's office was shut. Gina spotted me and waved me into her office.

"I'm so sorry," she said. "Something came up unexpectedly, and Lee's not here. He was wondering if you could meet with him at eight-thirty."

That was almost an hour and half from now. Although slightly annoyed, I nodded. "Sure. I actually have—"

A phone trilled from inside a small designer bag on Gina's desk.

"Excuse me," Gina said, smiling. She pulled out the phone. As she listened, her smile faded. "I'll be right there."

"I'm sorry." She stashed her phone back in her bag. "I have to go. Why don't you explore the grounds until it's time for your interview with Lee?"

She ushered me out of the building, locked the door, and rushed off.

Today was one of those special summer days on Long Island—not too hot and no humidity. I hoped the animals might be more active than they were in yesterday's heat. My tour with Nick Lamonica had been top notch, but sometimes you discover more when you're on your own.

As I made my way down the path, I was careful not to get too close to Manfred the llama. When Nick showed me Manfred yesterday, he told me the llama had been abused by his former owner who was known for poking the poor animal with a stick. As a result, Manfred spit at people passing by. His habitat had been set far enough away from the path so his saliva wouldn't reach anyone, but I wasn't about to take any chances.

Nick told me the other llamas in the habitat didn't spit and enjoyed human contact.

As I continued my stroll, I passed Sal the seagull. According to the brochure Gina gave me yesterday, Sal had been shot about a year ago. His wing was permanently damaged, and he could never fly again.

I glanced at my watch and saw it was eight-ten. Since it was a bit of a walk to the administration building, I had started heading back for my appointment with Lee Adler when I heard voices coming from behind a small shed. I recognized one of the voices. I snuck behind to look and listen.

"I know you want her job, and to tell the truth, I'd much prefer you," Nick Lamonica said.

"Why can't you just fire her?" asked the other man. I couldn't see his face, but he wore orange leather boots.

"Be patient Sam," Nick answered. "She may be gone sooner than you realize."

A woman's scream pierced the air.

CHAPTER 5

Nick and the man in orange boots sped off in the direction of the scream. I raced after them.

The scream had come from Gina Garone. She pointed toward one of the animal enclosures. Spread across the grass was a body. Hovering over the body was a mountain of fur with fangs.

Bella the bear.

Nick pulled out his radio communicator. "This is an emergency. Declan, we need you with your tranquilizer gun at the bear enclosure. Bring a gurney with wheels too."

Nick turned to the man in the orange boots and said, "I doubt it, but there's a chance the victim is still alive."

I stood next to Gina, who appeared in shock. She remained silent.

"What are you going to do?" I asked Nick.

Nick did a double take. I don't think he realized until now that I was here.

"I'm calling for medical help. They should be here by the time we secure Bella." Nick grabbed his phone, punched in a number, and requested assistance.

Within moments, Declan arrived in a pick-up truck.

"Once I shoot the tranquilizer, Bella should be out cold pretty quickly," Declan said. "She's up close, so she's in range."

Declan aimed. The dart hit Bella.

When the bear fell to the ground, Declan said, "Let's move her and lock her inside. I've the gurney in the truck."

"Sam and I can help." Nick pulled keys out of his pocket. The three men entered the exhibit through a small brick building located on the side of the bear enclosure. They emerged from this building into the open area of the habitat. They moved the tranquilized bear onto the gurney and then into the cave. The cave had a large steel door that they secured closed.

Nick ran to the body and knelt beside it.

"It's Maureen McDermott," Nick called out. "And she's dead."

CHAPTER 6

Seconds later, an ambulance careened to a stop in front of the bear habitat. A police car followed.

"It's too late," Nick yelled to the emergency medical technicians as they jumped out of their vehicle. "She's gone."

Two police officers hopped out of their car, and Nick directed them to the side entrance of the enclosure through the brick building. When the police reached Maureen's body, they began securing the crime scene and spoke briefly to Nick, as well as to Declan and the man in the orange boots whom Nick had referred to as Sam. A few minutes later, the three zoo employees exited the habitat.

"What's happening?" I asked once they reached where Gina and I stood.

"The officer told us to wait here," answered the man in the orange boots. "They'll want to question us."

"They'll need to talk to you too, Gina, since you were first on the scene," Nick added.

Gina frowned. "Why? She was killed by Bella?"

"I guess they still have to investigate how this happened." Nick shrugged.

"Isn't the bear locked away before a keeper enters an enclosure?" I asked.

"Yes. But there's more to this. Maureen had nothing to do

with the bear. She handled much smaller animals." Nick paused and frowned, his black, bushy brows melding together like a giant caterpillar. "She had no authorization to be here."

"We all know Maureen had problems with authority," Gina added.

"But how could she get inside then?" I asked.

"You can't expect a keeper to use fifty different keys, so the same key is used to gain access to all animal habitats. Maureen could enter any enclosure." Nick shook his head. "She just wasn't supposed to do so."

"Does anyone have keys besides the animal keepers?" I asked.

"I do," said Declan.

"There's a key in the main office too," Gina volunteered. "It's in the top drawer of the receptionist's desk."

The crime scene investigators and the medical examiner's staff arrived. As they checked out the body and surrounding ground, and we continued waiting, Nick introduced me to the man in orange boots. His name was Sam Garcia, and he was gorgeous—movie star gorgeous. He wasn't tall, but he was sleek with dark wavy hair and coffee-colored eyes. He was a part-time animal keeper.

Soon a police officer approached. With his heavy-set build, somewhat large ears, and big brown eyes, he reminded me of a Basset Hound. He introduced himself as Officer Callahan.

"This should be brief," he said. "Obviously the bear killed her, but there might be a case of negligence." He pulled out a pen and notepad. "I'll need to fill out a report. Who was the first one here to reach the body?"

"I guess it was me," Gina answered. "I'm Gina Garone, the director."

We all quickly introduced ourselves. "Sam and I heard Gina scream, although I didn't know who it was at the time," Nick said. "We came running. Then I called Declan, our veterinarian, to tranquilize the bear so we could get in."

The officer asked a few more questions and then stated, "The bear needs to be put down."

I felt pity for the bear. Up until five days ago, she spent her entire life in a cage with barely enough room to pace back and forth.

I knew Bella killed a human, but it didn't make sense. Why was a small animal keeper in the bear enclosure?

Before anyone could react, another police officer came running in our direction. She whispered in Officer Callahan's ear.

Officer Callahan shut his notebook, his face grim. "I'm sorry. You're all going to have to stay until the homicide detectives arrive."

"Why? Are they arresting Bella?" Nick asked, sarcastically.

"We still need to conduct an autopsy, but I've been informed it appears the victim may have been dead when the bear attacked her," Callahan replied. "The bear is not her killer."

CHAPTER 7

What seemed like an hour wait was only fifteen minutes. From the corner of my eye, I saw a Crown Victoria pull to a stop in front of the bear habitat. Two men in suits emerged. As they approached, I spotted badges hanging from their belts.

"Rats!" I muttered. I recognized the men as Detective Steve Wolfe and Detective Adrian Fox from the homicide bureau.

Detective Wolfe was a bully who had gone to school with my younger brother and had constantly picked on him. Granted my brother was the classic nerd who might as well have worn the sign, "Kick Me" on his back.

I also had solved three of Detective Wolfe's most recent cases, and that did not endear me to him.

Wolfe sported a receding hairline, blond mustache, and a pot belly. His upper body was puffed up like a lizard who wants to appear more menacing. He talked with the two police officers before he made his way to where our group stood.

"You!" He spotted me, and his face turned purple. "How come whenever you're around people die?"

Not the nicest way to put it.

"I'm doing a story on the animal sanctuary and—"

"And you just happened to be here when the body was discovered."

I nodded.

"Wait here," Wolfe ordered through gritted teeth. He and Fox left and talked briefly with the crime scene investigators. After a few minutes, they returned and spoke to our little group.

"We're going to talk to you all separately." Wolfe faced his partner and added, "You take Mrs. Farrell. Once she gives her statement, she needs to leave. I don't want her hanging around."

Detective Fox and I exchanged glances. Adrian Fox was a Black man in his early thirties. He was a smart detective, but, unfortunately, Wolfe was the senior partner who called the shots. And Wolfe never met a corner he didn't cut. Still, when a murder took place last spring at a nature refuge, Fox and I worked together without Wolfe's knowledge and solved the case.

"Let's go over here to talk." Detective Fox pointed to a nearby bench. We made our way to the bench and sat down.

"The crime scene investigators told us the body was still warm. When you heard the scream and raced over here, did you see anyone besides Gina Garone near the enclosure?" he asked.

"I didn't see a soul." But his comment struck a chord, and I repeated it. "You said the body was still warm. How long ago did the murder occur?"

Fox looked around, probably to ensure that Wolfe wasn't in hearing distance. Wolfe didn't like it when Fox shared news with me about a murder.

"It won't be official until the autopsy, but we're pretty sure she was killed within an hour of the time the body was discovered," he said.

I shuddered as I realized how close I might have been when the murder occurred.

Access to the sanctuary was only through the main gate

which had a guard and a security camera. The sanctuary was open to the public two days a month, but this was not one of them.

This meant the killer had to be someone who worked here.

CHAPTER 8

"The murder is all over the news," Abby said as she burst into my kitchen that evening. She knelt down to greet Brandy and Archie who now provided her with a thorough face licking. "You were there, Mom, right?"

I nodded. "I was one of the first on the scene."

Abby stretched and grabbed a wine glass from the top cabinet. Only a little more than five feet tall, she inherited her height genes from me. She poured a glass of wine, pulled out a chair, and settled down at the table across from where I had been working on my story. I put my laptop aside and told her all that happened.

"What are you thinking?" I asked when I noticed my daughter scowling.

"I'm worried the police will accuse Declan."

I had thought that too. With Maureen McDermott out of the picture, there now would be no formal charges against Declan.

"He can't be the only one with a motive to kill her," I said.

"Declan told me everyone hated her. She was nasty to all." Abby sipped her wine.

"Nastiness isn't a reason to kill someone."

"The accusation she made against Declan was a lie. If she lied about him, maybe she lied and spread rumors about others too," Abby argued.

Before I could speak, the two dogs, who had been resting on either side of Abby, rose from their spots and raced to the door.

"Here's dinner." My husband, Matt, strolled into the kitchen carrying a large pizza box, a salad, and a paper bag that by the smell I knew contained garlic knots.

"Jason just texted me," Abby said, glancing at her phone. "He should be here in five minutes."

I decided to put the murder on the back burner—temporarily. "How are you and Jason coming along with the plans for the wedding?"

"Fine, except for grandma's suggestions. I love her, but she's a bit…"

"Opinionated." I completed the thought.

"She constantly texts me. She wants Aunt Varcia and Aunt Melita seated at the same table. They haven't spoken in three years. Grandma believes if they're together at a happy occasion, like a wedding, they'll make up. I don't agree."

"Me either." I paused. "Grandma will be here on Sunday." My widowed mother, who lived in Florida, always came up for a visit in mid-July and stayed through Labor Day.

"I know." Abby groaned. "She told me once she arrives, we can have weekly wedding planning meetings."

I stifled a smile. "I'll talk to her. I'm sure—"

The dogs interrupted me with their barks as they scampered to the door again. This time, Jason burst into the room, cake box in hand. "Dessert. It's chocolate cake."

Since there was nothing I could do about my mother's interference until she arrived on Sunday, I decided to steer the conversation back to the murder. My daughter's fiancé was an assistant district attorney. Although he worked in white collar crime, his contacts proved helpful in the previous murders I'd solved. I was hoping he could help now.

"Any news about Maureen McDermott's autopsy?" I asked.

He grinned. "I knew that would be the first thing you'd say. No. It's too soon. But the bear wounds were definitely inflicted after the victim was dead."

"Any suspects?" Abby questioned. Her voice quivered ever so slightly. I knew she worried about Declan.

"I haven't heard anything yet." Jason pulled open the refrigerator door and grabbed a beer.

We sat around the table and ate the pizza. The two dogs hovered near my feet since I was the most likely to feed them crust.

"When I was at the sanctuary, I got the feeling that the director disliked Maureen. That makes me curious as to how Maureen got hired." I turned toward my daughter. "Did Declan ever say anything?"

Abby smiled. "Declan told me a lot about the sanctuary, including how various members of the staff were hired. Maureen was interviewed for her job by both the director, Gina Garone, and head animal keeper, Jack Scranton—"

"Whoa!" I interrupted. "Who's Jack Scranton? Nick Lamonica is the head animal keeper."

"Jack was the original head animal keeper. Unfortunately, Jack was in a bad car accident and needed to leave the job permanently. Gina hired Nick as Jack's replacement. Nick's only been there three months."

"So Maureen was there before Nick. Do you think Maureen was jealous because she didn't get promoted to head animal keeper?" I thought about the animosity between Nick and Maureen on the day I first visited the sanctuary.

Abby shook her head. "No. Maureen wasn't qualified to be a head animal keeper. She had no experience with big, dangerous animals which is a requirement for the top job."

"I'm still surprised Gina hired Maureen. They didn't appear to get along." I palmed two pieces of pizza crust to the dogs.

"Declan told me the chair of the board of trustees, Carolyn Whitcome, recommended Maureen."

"A director is usually predisposed toward a 'recommendation' from the chair of the board." I grinned.

We all sat silently for a few seconds. Dozens of questions whipped through my mind, but two kept reappearing.

What was Carolyn Whitcome's connection to Maureen McDermott?

Why was there friction between the victim and others on the staff? It had to be caused by more than her nastiness?

Abby broke the silence. "What are you thinking, Mom?"

"I think the first thing I need to do is find out more about Maureen."

"We know the staff disliked her. But it seems to be only because she was a cranky person," Abby said.

"True. But things aren't always as they seem. People often show you only what they want you to see."

Abby nodded in agreement. "I'll bet if you dig deep enough, you'll uncover motives for wanting her dead."

CHAPTER 9

The next morning, when I arrived at the Happy Place Animal Sanctuary, the first person I ran into was Nick Lamonica. He was pushing a wheelbarrow full of fruit—peaches, apples, blueberries, grapes, and bananas.

"Do you have a minute?" I asked.

"No more than one minute. We're short staffed, and the animals need to eat."

"The killer either murdered Maureen in the bear enclosure or killed her elsewhere and then dragged the body into the exhibit, right?" I asked.

Nick nodded. "That's how it appears."

"How come the bear didn't attack the killer?"

"Because Bella was locked up until the killer left. I've started studying the bear's sleep patterns, so she's locked in the cave for the night, where video cameras record her actions. I release her the next morning, usually between eight-fifteen and eight-thirty."

He paused. "This is my theory. Whoever killed Maureen either murdered her in the bear habitat or dropped her dead body there later. This would have been done while the bear was in the cave. Then the killer entered the brick building on the side where the control panel is located and pressed the button to raise the steel door, releasing Bella. Once the bear was out, the killer exited through the brick building which has an entrance to the outside."

"There are video cameras?" I asked.

"Inside the cave—for my research. When we raise more money, we hope to install several outside. Right now, the only other cameras in the sanctuary are at the security station by the main gate." He glanced at his watch. "I have to get back to work."

Minutes later, I stepped into the administration building. I didn't have an appointment. This was a surprise visit, but luckily I found Gina Garone in her office.

"Gina," I called.

She looked up and motioned me into her office. "I know you never got to interview Lee Adler after all that happened yesterday," she said. "He's in Manhattan today at an office supplies exposition. Perhaps we can set up a meeting for tomorrow. I can call him—"

"That would be great. But I wanted to talk to you too." I slid into a chair facing her desk although she hadn't asked me to sit down.

"I thought we finished our interview," Gina said.

"I want to talk to you about Maureen McDermott."

Gina frowned, but before she could respond, I spoke up. "I'd like to hear your side of the story. Why did you hire her?"

Gina pursed her lips. I wasn't sure she would answer, but she did.

"I hired her because of her qualifications," Gina spoke slowly, apparently choosing her words carefully. "Maureen graduated top of her class with a degree in animal science."

"What about work experience? Was she employed at another sanctuary or zoo before coming here?" I asked. "Maureen appeared to be in her late fifties, so I assume her graduation happened a while back."

"No. She only graduated a year ago. This was her second career."

"What did she do before?"

"She was a divorce lawyer."

"What!" I couldn't believe I heard correctly.

Gina leaned back in her chair. "Eight years ago—she was fifty at the time—Maureen married for the first time. Two years later, she developed breast cancer. Six months after that, while still undergoing chemotherapy, her husband had a massive heart attack and died."

Maybe there was a reason she was so miserable, I thought.

Gina sat back. "Anyway, those two events had a life changing effect on her. Maureen always loved animals. She had enough money to live comfortably, so once her treatment was finished and she was cancer free, she went back to school to pursue a degree in animal science. She'd taken courses in that field earlier in her life and had a few credits that still applied. She got her degree in three years."

I sat silently for a moment, soaking this in. "I heard Carolyn Whitcome, chair of your board or trustees, recommended her for the job. How did she know Maureen?"

"Maureen handled Carolyn's divorce from her first husband." Gina quickly added, "Carolyn told me Maureen was a super smart lady who graduated the top of her class. The sanctuary was scheduled to open in two weeks, so we needed to hire someone immediately."

"But her people skills were lacking. How did you feel about that?"

"She was fine during the interview." Gina shrugged. "She wasn't the warmest person, but she was polite."

"So, it was after you hired her when the friction occurred?"

Gina frowned. "I wouldn't call it friction. Maureen was passionate about her work, and sometimes that made her goals unrealistic. She didn't have a great deal of tact."

Earlier in the week, when Maureen confronted Gina in the office, it certainly looked like friction to me.

"Shall I make an appointment for you to interview Lee?" Gina asked, changing the subject.

"That would be great."

Gina reached Lee and set up a meeting for mid-morning tomorrow. I figured I'd gotten all I was going to get from Gina and was about to leave when a voice called out from the reception area.

"Good morning, Gina. With all that happened, I wanted to see how you were doing."

I turned my head as a statuesque blond with Viking coloring strutted into the room. She had the unmistakable look of someone born to wealth and privilege. She appeared to be in her late thirties, and she wore her hair in an elegant French twist.

The woman continued speaking. "I thought we could… Oh, I'm sorry. I didn't realize you were with someone."

"This is Kristy Farrell, writer for *Animal Advocate Magazine*," Gina said. "Kristy, this is our chair of the board of trustees, Carolyn Whitcome."

"A journalist." Carolyn's body tensed and her face darkened. "Are you writing about what happened to Maureen?"

"Since it is news, I may include a mention of what happened—probably a sidebar. I'm not sure about that yet. But my major focus is on the sanctuary and the work it does in rescuing animals."

"Kristy was asking me why we hired Maureen," Gina said to Carolyn. "I told her—"

"I have an idea." Carolyn didn't wait for Gina to finish. "Why don't I take Kristy to lunch? I can tell her how the sanctuary started and the rigorous procedure we went through in hiring staff."

"Sounds great." I needed to dig into the lives of the sanctuary staff, especially Maureen McDermott. While I was telling the truth—the murder was not the major focus of my story, I was not about to let Declan take a fall for a crime that he didn't commit.

And I hoped he didn't commit it.

CHAPTER 10

Carolyn suggested her sailing club for lunch, which was located only ten minutes away from the animal sanctuary.

"Let's eat outside," Carolyn said once we pulled up in front of the building, and the valet took her car.

The club's outdoor dining patio overlooked a harbor on the Long Island Sound. We were seated at a table with an excellent view of dozens of sailboats moored offshore. I sat back and relaxed for a moment as I inhaled the smell of salt water wafting through the breeze.

"That belongs to my husband Bradford," Carolyn said, pointing to one of the largest boats in the water."

"Do you go out on it a lot?"

Carolyn shook her head. "Brad does, but I'm not into sailing. My love is horses and riding. That's where Gina and I met. We both board our horses at the Mayfair Stables. We've been friends for nearly two decades."

After placing our orders—two shrimp salads and iced tea— Carolyn began talking about the sanctuary. Although she was chair of the board of trustees, she also volunteered for special events at the sanctuary, so she knew everyone who worked there. When she started filling me in on staff, I saw my opportunity to focus the conversation on Maureen McDermott.

"From attorney to animal keeper—that's an unusual

turnabout," I said.

"Not really. Lots of people change careers. After years of working in a high paying but boring or stressful job, they do what they've always dreamt of doing."

We paused while the server delivered our iced teas. Carolyn took a sip and then continued. "Divorce law is grueling. Maureen aspired to be a judge, but she was denied the opportunity."

"Why?" I wondered if this was a motive for murder, but I dismissed that thought as I remembered she had to be killed by someone with access to the sanctuary. Aside from me, I was pretty sure the only people on the property when she was murdered were employees—and as far as I knew that didn't include any lawyers.

"I don't know why she was denied a judgeship, but in her line of work, I'm sure she made lots of enemies. I heard someone in the bar association had enough political clout to keep her off the bench." Carolyn shrugged. "But since her real love was animals, she chose a second career in this field."

"Gina seemed to despise Maureen." I told Carolyn about the argument I witnessed between the two women. Maybe "despise" was too strong, but I was anxious to see Carolyn's reaction.

"In the beginning, Gina was impressed with Maureen. But about two months ago, Gina did a total turnabout. Suddenly, she was constantly criticizing her," Carolyn said.

"What happened?"

"I don't know. It occurred at the time of Gina's father's funeral. At first, I thought Gina was on edge because of her dad's sudden death. Now I think there was more to it."

Carolyn and Gina were friends. If I made Carolyn believe I thought Gina was guilty, maybe Carolyn would attempt to divert suspicion away from Gina to another employee. And she might do this by feeding me information about the rest of the staff.

"Gina certainly had motive and opportunity to murder Maureen," I said.

Carolyn changed gears in an instant. Her smiling face morphed into a frown. "It's a big stretch from criticizing Maureen to killing her. They may not have liked each other, but there's no way Gina would murder Maureen."

"Tell me, who do you think killed her?" I leaned forward.

"The most obvious suspect is Declan. Maureen hated him, but he claimed he had no idea why she held such animosity toward him. He said the first time they met was at the sanctuary, but I don't believe that. They had to have some history together."

Carolyn continued talking, ignoring the fact that the server was placing our meals in from of us. "I assume you heard about the accusation Maureen made against Declan. That's one reason everyone is looking at him for the murder."

I shook my head. "I know Declan. I don't believe he's capable of killing anyone."

"Other staff had problems too," Carolyn added quickly. "Gina told me Sam Garcia was always badmouthing Maureen."

"Why?"

Carolyn shrugged. "I don't think it was anything in particular. Maureen had a difficult personality. She rubbed people the wrong way."

"But you don't kill for that," I said. "What about Lee and Nick?"

"Lee never talked about her one way or the other. But I could tell he didn't like her."

"How could you tell?" I sipped my iced tea.

"Lee's the business manager. Staff submits expenses to him. And Lee always questioned receipts from Maureen."

"Maybe she was a sloppy record keeper."

"I doubt that. Maureen was meticulous in all she did." Carolyn took a forkful of shrimp and finished chewing before speaking again. "There's more. Lee appeared to take more time ordering her supplies than for anyone else. It's like he was taunting her."

"That sounds strange."

"I've no idea why he acted that way. Some people like to be annoying. As far as I knew, they never had a nasty argument. According to Gina, whenever Maureen complained to Lee—and she did that a lot—Lee would just nod and say he'd work on the problem. That made Maureen even angrier."

"What about Nick?"

"Of course, Nick hated her," Carolyn said as if the reason would be obvious.

The reason wasn't obvious to me, so I stared at her quizzically.

"Maureen McDermott was the divorce lawyer for Nick's ex-wife," Carolyn said. "She raked him over the coals and took him for everything he had, including the kids. When he was hired and found out that Maureen was working here, he went ballistic."

CHAPTER 11

Abby burst through my kitchen door. Archie and Brandy scampered into the room to greet her.

"I wasn't expecting you tonight," I glanced at the clock. It was almost ten. I'd been sitting at the table in my pajamas researching Maureen McDermott. "Is everything okay?"

Abby pulled up a chair across from me. She gave no attention to the dogs which was totally out of character. In their minds, my daughter was always good for a back scratch or tummy rub.

"We need to talk about grandma and the wedding."

"Oh boy!" I put my laptop aside.

"Do you know grandma's latest idea? She wants me to color coordinate the bridesmaid dresses with the dessert. She told me not to serve a chocolate wedding cake because brown goes best with fall colors, and I'm having a spring wedding."

"There are other earth tones that go with chocolate—"

"MOM!"

"Just teasing. Grandma will be here Sunday. I promise we'll sit and talk with her."

"Probably at the weekly wedding planning meeting she expects to hold," Abby mumbled. "I don't want to hurt her feelings but—"

The trilling of Abby's phone interrupted the conversation.

"Oh, no. That's not good," she said. Her voice sounded

distraught.

"What's wrong?" I asked when she finished her call.

"That was Jason with the preliminary findings of Maureen McDermott's autopsy. The cause of death was a lethal dose of a drug called etorphine." She paused. "Etorphine is a common anesthesia for large animals, like elephants or bears."

I sucked in my breath. An anesthesia would be a controlled substance, and Declan would have legal access to it.

I told Abby about Maureen's previous legal career. She hadn't known.

"Declan never mentioned it," she said. "I'll bet he wasn't aware she had once worked as a divorce lawyer."

I was about to make another comment when the dogs, who by now had settled on either side of Abby, suddenly rose and darted to the door. Within seconds, the doorbell rang.

"Are you expecting someone?" Abby asked.

"Not at all."

I rose from my chair and made my way across the room with trepidation. Who would drop by late at night without calling first? I had my suspicions since this did happen once before.

The bell rang again. Whoever was there was impatient.

I peeked out the side window. "I was right," I muttered as I swung open the door.

There she stood. A woman in her early seventies, who at first glance appeared at least fifteen years younger, with short, blond hair and creamy skin. She was perfectly made up and wearing a floral sundress and low heeled white sandals that showed off her pastel pink toenails. "Mom!"

"Are you going to let me in?"

"Of course." I moved aside and my mother, Mary Frances O'Hara Vanikos, paraded into the house. I noticed she held a pet carrier. Brandy and Archie noticed it too and were sniffing it. Suddenly, a paw darted out through the front of the carrier in an attempt to reach Archie's nose. The dog whined and backed up.

"What's in there?" I asked.

"Merlin. My Siamese cat."

My mother placed the carrier on the floor and kissed Abby and I hello.

"You look surprised, Kristy," she said.

"I expected you on Sunday."

"I know. But I need your help, and I need it before Sunday."

CHAPTER 12

As anxious as I was to find out why my mother needed to see us before Sunday, I had to first take care of the "Merlin" situation.

"When did you get the cat?" I asked, peeking in the carrier.

"Two months ago. Didn't I mention it during one of our phone calls?"

"No. You did not."

"The local shelter sponsored a booth at our town's spring festival. I saw him, and it was love at first sight."

I smiled. I understood perfectly. But I suddenly remembered something else, and my smile faded. "Your condo doesn't allow pets."

Mom's face clouded. "You're right. Since Merlin is an indoor cat, I thought no one except my close friends would know. But Merlin has this habit of sunning himself in my window."

Cats are like that.

"Old Mister Franklin spotted him," my mother went on to say. "He reported it to the condo association."

Old Mister Franklin was ten years younger than my mother. I thought it best not to mention that.

"So what are you going to do?" I asked.

"I thought you might take him—"

"What! But—"

"I won't take him back to the shelter."

"Of course. We need to make sure he has a good home, but—"

"You have dogs," my mother interrupted. "You need a cat. Cats keep you humble."

Did that come from a fortune cookie? And I didn't know my mom thought I needed humility.

"We have to find out how Merlin gets along with Archie and Brandy," I said, firmly.

"Merlin loves dogs," my mother quickly added.

"He tried to swat Archie."

"That's because he's caged. Once loose, he'll be fine."

I hoped this would work. I'm a sucker for animals. Our last cat, Gus, passed away a few months ago, and I missed him terribly.

Abby suggested we introduce one dog at a time. We started with Brandy who was the calmer of the two canines. Then we introduced Archie. After the traditional butt sniffing, the two dogs stretched out on the floor with their bones, and Merlin padded off to the living room to explore his new surroundings. Success!

"What's going on? Did a cat scoot by me?" My husband stepped into the kitchen with a confused expression on his face. He'd been in the den watching the Yankees game. He saw my mom, hugged her, then said, "I thought—"

"You thought I was coming Sunday." My mother handed Matt her keys. "My suitcases are in my rental car. Would you be a dear and put them in the guest room? Then hurry back here. We all need to talk."

CHAPTER 13

I poured wine and we huddled around the kitchen table. Merlin had taken to me and was now curled up on my lap.

"Why must you talk to us before Sunday?" I asked. "What's wrong?"

"Nothing's wrong. I have a fabulous opportunity for Matt."

I exchanged glances with Abby and Matt.

"Do you remember Marcia Silver?" my mom asked.

We all nodded. My mother and Marcia had been neighbors on Long Island and good friends for more than forty years. Marcia was now a snowbird and wintered in the same condo complex in Florida where my mother lived. Marcia had been back on Long Island since the beginning of April.

"Marcia invested in a new business," my mother went on to say. "Marcia is selling pet supplies for Ajax Pet Products. This would be a perfect side business for Matt. You should buy a franchise."

"I don't think so. I'm a veterinarian not a salesperson. But I'd be happy to look at your friend's merchandise if that would help. Perhaps there are items I could use in my practice."

My mother shook her head. "She doesn't make much money selling products. There is a catalog, but the Ajax Company actually discourages its representatives from pushing any of the items. Marcia's sales manager says it's a waste of time. The big money is made in selling franchises."

She paused to catch her breath and then added, "You know other veterinarians, right? And I'm sure you have contacts with people involved in animal organizations. Your clients probably have lots of friends with pets, too."

She continued, not waiting for anyone to reply. "For each franchise you sell, you make a commission. And if anyone who buys a franchise from you sells franchises to anyone else, you get a cut of that too—just like Marcia would get a cut based on what you sell. Then, if the person you sell to—"

"Grandma, that sounds like a pyramid scheme," Abby interrupted.

"A what?"

"It's when an investor recruits other investors, who in turn recruit more investors. It's a scam that always bottoms out. The later investors are never able to sell enough franchises to recoup their money."

My mother frowned. "Agree to differ. I think it depends how much effort you put into selling."

"But Grandma…"

I shot Abby a look and shook my head. My mother was stubborn. It definitely sounded like a pyramid scheme. But we would need a lot more proof to convince her—proof we could get but didn't have at our fingertips.

"The monthly dinner and sales meeting of Ajax Pet Products is this Sunday," my mom said, ignoring our distressed faces. "Marcia hasn't sold any franchise yet, so it would be fabulous if you could go to this meeting, and she could introduce you as a potential buyer. It's a wonderful opportunity for you too."

"No. This isn't a good idea," Matt said.

"At least talk to Marcia." My mother frowned again.

Matt shook his head.

"Dad, I think grandma is right. We should hear Marcia's

side."

Why did Abby have this sudden change of attitude? I turned toward her with a puzzled look.

"I have my reasons." Abby whispered to Matt and me.

Matt nodded although he did not look pleased. "Okay. I'll meet with Marcia. But no promises."

"Good." My mother smiled. "I'll arrange a get together with Marcia for tomorrow evening so you can talk to her before Sunday's dinner meeting. You should all come. Is that good?"

Abby pulled out her phone and held it under the table out of view, but I could see her fingers texting.

After checking our schedules, we all agreed to the meeting with Marcia Silver. My mother excused herself to go unpack.

"Okay Abby. What's this about?" I asked once my mom was out of earshot.

"Dad is savvy enough not to get involved in a pyramid scam where we would only lose our money. But there are lots of people out there who will fall for this scheme."

"Marcia already has," Matt said. "She could lose her entire investment."

"Right." Abby nodded. "So we need to stop this. When we meet with Marcia tomorrow, I'm bringing Jason. We had planned to go to dinner tomorrow night, so I know he's free. I just sent him a text. Hopefully, his white collar crime unit at the District Attorney's office can get involved."

Abby turned to face me. "Mom since this scam involves animal supplies you might want to write an article for your magazine."

I'd need to run it by my editor, but it was a good idea.

For the present time there was nothing more to say about the pyramid scam. Realizing I hadn't finished questioning Abby about Maureen McDermott's autopsy, I returned to that.

"Does Jason know yet if Maureen's murder occurred in the

bear habitat or was the body moved there?" I asked, quickly switching topics.

"He didn't say. But he confirmed that when the body was found, Maureen had been dead less than an hour."

"The sanctuary doesn't have many employees. We need to find out who was there at that time."

"Can you do that?" Abby asked.

"I think so. I'm sure the police will check the camera by the entrance booth where the security guard sits. I'll call Detective Fox in the morning and see what he knows."

As I sipped my wine, I pondered what I knew. Lee missed his seven-fifteen appointment with me because "something came up," and Gina suddenly was called away from her office.

Where did they go?

Could either of them have murdered Maureen McDermott?

"After you speak to Detective Fox, what's your next course of action?" Abby asked me. "I assume you'll want to check each suspect for motive, means, and opportunity."

"Absolutely. And I need to expand my search of Maureen McDermott. There's lots of information from when she was a lawyer, but aside from the sanctuary web page, there's nothing about her career with animals."

"What more could you possibly hope to find?"

I shrugged. "I don't know exactly. But if you know about a murder victim, it should tell you something about who committed the murder."

CHAPTER 14

The next day, back at the sanctuary, the first person I spotted was Sam Garcia. He was still wearing his orange boots.

Sam was filling up the food troughs for the donkeys. He was flanked by two of these animals.

"These donkeys are the sweetest creatures. Their names are Oliver and Tobias," Sam told me as he shook his head. "They'd been abused by their owner."

"How were they abused?"

"These were once wild donkeys, but they were captured and sold. Their owner beat them on a regular basis. They were finally taken away by the authorities when a neighbor spotted the owner and three of his cronies, who were all drunk. They were climbing atop Oliver. The poor donkey collapsed from the pressure."

Oliver raised his head from the food trough and nuzzled Sam.

"I can tell these animals love you, and you love them," I said. "Nick mentioned you're part-time. How frequently do you work here?"

Sam grinned, showing teeth worthy of a television newscaster. He really was sexy looking. "I'm full time now. With Maureen gone, I've been bumped up."

I flashed back to the conversation between Nick and Sam

prior to discovering Maureen's body. Sam had been pushing Nick for Maureen's job. Now he had it.

"It's funny how things work out," he continued. "I always loved animals. As a kid, my home was a haven for strays. I took a few animal science courses at college too. But I worked for my father's restaurant, El Mar, which had a five-star rating. He and I both assumed I'd take over when he retired."

"What happened?"

"The restaurant closed. My father sold the building, and it reopened under another name with a new owner."

I wondered what would cause a five-star restaurant to close.

"Was it Covid related?" A lot of restaurants never recovered from the economic loss during the pandemic.

"No. It was personal reasons," he mumbled as he averted my eyes and stared at his feet. "It involved my dad's health—his heart." Sam rubbed his face with his hand.

As a former teacher, I could tell when someone was lying. I wasn't sure if what Sam said was true, but I knew he wasn't telling the whole story.

But since I didn't think his dad's restaurant had anything to do with the murder, I changed the subject.

"How did you wind up here?" I asked.

"My uncle owns the stable where Gina Garone and Carolyn Whitcome board their horses. I've helped out there part-time since I was a teenager. When the sanctuary opened, Gina and Carolyn offered me a job here. But I still work special events with the horses on my days off from the sanctuary."

"Sometimes things work out for the best. You seem to love working here."

"I do." He smiled. "I like working with animals a lot more than I liked working in the food industry."

"I think you're a big asset," I then changed the subject. "I heard lots of the staff didn't get along with Maureen. How about you?"

Sam's face darkened. "I didn't like her. She was bossy and sarcastic. Do you know she never said please or thank you?"

He sighed and shook his head. "I better get going now. I need to hide treats for the monkeys. After that, I have a fence to fix."

Sam made his way toward the back of the donkey enclosure. Oliver and Tobias, who had finished their meal, trailed behind him. As I departed and made my way to the administration building, I thought about his comment.

But no one killed someone because they didn't say please or thank you.

Right?

Lee was behind his desk when I arrived.

"Good. You're on time," he said, motioning me to a seat. His smile was polite rather than friendly. "How can I help you?"

We got right down to business. He answered my questions.

"Do you have an annual report?" I asked when I was almost finished with the interview. "If so, I'd like a copy."

"I think Gina has a few in her office. I'll go get one."

Once he left the room, I stood up and surveyed the top of his desk. As a reporter, I sometimes picked up useful information this way.

Aside from a computer, office phone, notepad, and pen, there were only three other items. Two were bills—one from the Relda Animal Supplies Corporation and the other from the power company that provided the electricity. The third item was a written request from Declan for a key to the equipment storage facility. Nothing here that I thought could help me with my story.

I heard footsteps, so I quickly returned to my seat.

"Here you go." Lee stepped back into the room and handed

me the annual report. I stashed it in my bag for later and continued with my questions.

"Can you tell me something about your background? Gina told me you're a whiz with numbers."

"The left side of my brain is definitely in control. I'm a math person." He sat back, appearing to relax for the first time. "I'm currently attending Harper University with a dual major in accounting and business management—"

"You don't have your degree yet?"

"I'm almost finished. I worked for years in my father's jewelry business. Gina and her husband bought several items from us. We got to know each other, so she was aware of my abilities. That's why she hired me."

He smiled. "Since I haven't graduated yet, I can't command the same salary as someone with a degree. It's a savings for the sanctuary."

"What will happen when you finish at Harper?"

"I haven't decided. Non-profits never pay as much as private companies, but I like working here. I'm currently taking classes, Gina is flexible about my schedule, and this job looks great on my resume. Working here is right for me—for the present time."

He glanced at his watch. "If there is nothing else, I have several phone calls I need to make and—"

"I'm almost done." I assured him. "You said that the sanctuary is an expensive operation. What if Gina falls short with her fundraising and doesn't raise all the money needed to cover costs?"

"In that case, we need to cut our budget."

"How do you decide where to cut?"

"I would consult with staff, but I'd make the final decision." He brushed away a wisp of his sandy blond hair that had fallen on his forehead. "This could involve repairing rather than replacing broken equipment. It could also mean limiting the number of new animals we take."

"You'd make the decision? Not the director?"

"We would consult together. But Gina relies on me to do the budgeting while she handles raising the money."

"Have you needed to take any drastic measures yet?"

"We've done a lot of fixing and maintaining of what we have rather than buying new. But so far, we haven't refused any new animal." He tapped a pencil on his desk. "Unfortunately, with rising costs, it may come to that soon."

"I imagine that will be hard on the employees. From what I've seen, everyone here seems to love animals. They want to help as many as possible."

He shrugged. "Our staff is professional. They realize it has to be done."

"What about Maureen McDermott? I heard she could be difficult. Did you ever need to deny her requests?"

"Yes. Maureen was never happy with any decision involving budget cuts, and she was vocal about it."

That was all he said. Unlike the other employees, it appeared that Lee was not going to complain about Maureen.

Lee pushed his glasses up the bridge of his nose and glanced again at his watch. "If there's nothing else."

"Yes. I know you're busy. You had to postpone our last meeting because of an emergency." I smiled.

He didn't smile back, and he didn't respond.

"Gina told me you had something come up unexpectedly that morning. Is everything okay?" I asked, hoping he might tell me his whereabouts when Maureen was killed.

"Everything is fine." He rose from his chair. "Thanks for coming."

As I headed back to the parking lot, I spotted Declan hurrying up the path.

His pace was almost a run. With his head down, we might

collide.

"Declan!" I called, jumping to the side.

He jerked up his head and stopped short.

"I'm sorry," he said. "I should have watched where I was going.

"Are you okay?"

"No." He shook his head. "The police were at my veterinary infirmary. They had a search warrant."

I gasped. "What were they looking for?"

"Etorphine." He paused as he wiped the sweat from his forehead. "And some of mine is missing."

CHAPTER 15

"Missing? How could it be missing?"

Declan shook his head. "I don't know. It's a controlled substance, so I account for every bit I use. My records have to match my inventory."

"But you're saying this time they didn't."

"Right, but I didn't misplace it. I used some two weeks ago, and I recorded what remained. But now some is gone."

"What could have happened?

"I've no idea. Maybe someone took the drugs to frame me. Maybe someone wants me fired for not being careful."

"I'm afraid it's more than that." I had knowledge of the autopsy findings through my future son-in-law who served as an assistant district attorney, but these findings weren't public yet. Declan didn't know that etorphine killed Maureen McDermott.

Or did he?

As I told Declan about the autopsy, his eyes widened and his face validated my gut instinct. I was sure he hadn't been aware etorphine was the murder weapon.

"I'm a suspect, aren't I?" he asked.

I nodded, but I didn't say he was probably the number one suspect.

"Does anyone have access to your medicines?" I asked.

"The door to the infirmary is always locked when I'm away."

"What about when you're working there?"

"When I'm inside the building, staff comes in and out, but the medicine cabinet is always locked unless I'm using it." He ran his hand through his hair. "What should I do?"

"Discovering who took your medicine would go a long way to finding the killer."

Declan departed. A few seconds later, I spotted Nick headed in my direction, pushing a wheelbarrow full of hay.

"How are you making out without Maureen?" I asked.

"Sam's replaced her—he's full time now, and I'm interviewing candidates for his former part-time position. But until I hire someone, we're short staffed and all working extra duty."

He wiped the perspiration off his head. The temperature was nearly ninety.

"It couldn't come at a worst time," he continued to say. "My ex-wife, Teresa, is in town for a sales conference, and she brought the kids with her. They're staying with me. They're fifteen and sixteen, so they're old enough to be alone in my apartment. But since I rarely see them, I was looking forward to taking time off and spending it with them."

He frowned. "My wife is really annoyed too. It's not that she's mother of the year. She rarely has time for the kids with her job. The only reason she fought for custody is child support."

"What does your wife do for a living?" I asked.

"Teresa is a sales representative for Omega Animal Grooming Supplies. She sells wholesale to pet shops, big box stores, large veterinary practices, and pet grooming businesses."

I was familiar with the company. In the past, Matt had ordered a few supplies from Omega. He always thought they were top quality.

An idea popped up. I could kill two birds with one stone. I

hated that expression, but right now it fit.

First, I wanted to talk to Nick's wife about the divorce, hoping she could provide insight into the depth of anger Nick held toward her divorce attorney, Maureen McDermott.

The other reason for meeting Teresa involved my mother's friend Marcia Silver and her Ajax Pet Products pyramid scheme. Since Omega Animal Grooming Supplies was a respected corporation in the animal care industry, perhaps Nick's ex-wife knew of Ajax Pet Products and could provide information helpful in exposing them as a fraud.

It was a long shot but worth a try.

"Where is your ex-wife's conference being held?" I asked.

"In Manhattan. At the Bancroft Hotel. Why do you ask?"

"My husband owns a veterinary practice." I quickly racked my mind for an answer Nick would accept. "He's looking into putting in a line of grooming products. Lots of veterinarians are selling merchandise now. I would be interested in hearing what your wife's company has to offer."

"Give her a call. We may have less than a friendly relationship, but her products are first rate. If you meet with her, she'll probably want your husband there too since it's his business." Nick grinned. "She can be a bit impatient and only wants to deal with the person who has the authority to make purchasing decisions."

"My husband can't always get away, but my daughter Abby is also a veterinarian. She works for her dad, and she would be able to make purchases on behalf of the veterinary office. I'll bring her along."

He pulled out his phone. He texted me Teresa's cell number.

"Since you said your relationship with your wife is less than friendly, is it okay for me to say you gave me her contact information?" I asked.

"We've been divorced for more than seven years. Our

relationship has gotten better over time. We're cordial."

He sighed. "When we split up it was because we had grown apart. We fell out of love, but I thought we were still friends. I love my kids and planned to provide what I thought were generous monthly support payments. But she raked me over the coals."

I didn't think he expected a comment, so I waited.

"My ex-wife hired a hot shot lawyer," he finally continued. "At the time, I was employed by a small zoo. To keep up with the child support, I was forced to move into one room in a boarding house. I had to sell my car and take the bus to work. I didn't have enough to pay my health insurance premium and had to drop it. And several times for dinner, I ate spaghetti doused with ketchup."

The divorce happened long ago. He apparently was not aware that I knew his ex-wife's attorney was Maureen McDermott.

I stayed silent. I wanted him to keep on talking, and he did.

"A few years ago, my aunt died and left me a small amount of money. It was enough so I could move into an apartment and buy an old used car. Teresa spends more on designer clothing in one month than I spend on my rent. And she makes more than three times my salary."

Nick clenched his fists. I noticed how big his hands were.

An image still flashed through my mind.

I reminded myself that Maureen was killed by drugs and not strangled.

Still, I couldn't help picture those hands around Maureen McDermott's neck.

The man had a lot of pent up anger.

CHAPTER 16

I sped off to the *Animal Advocate Magazine* office and was greeted by Clara Schultheis, resident gossip and conspiracy theorist. She was also administrative assistant to the editor.

"Kristy, I've been waiting for you," she called from her desk, located a few feet from the front door. "What's the scoop on the murder at the sanctuary?" She didn't wait for my reply but immediately added, "Want to hear my theory?"

I didn't. I feared her theory might include aliens or werewolves.

"Maybe later," I called as I scooted around Clara's desk and grabbed a mug of coffee. Once I made my way to my cubicle, I phoned Teresa Lamonica and arranged a meeting for later today. I also called Abby. I knew she was operating on a Great Dane this morning, so I left a message for her to get back to me.

My final call was to the private cell number for Detective Fox. He had given me this number so I could avoid calls to headquarters where Detective Wolfe might find out what I was doing.

It went straight to voice mail and I left a message. Next, I booted up my computer. Until Fox returned my call, I would check on the people I knew were at the sanctuary when the murder occurred.

The first person on my list was Gina Garone. Since Gina and

her husband were socially prominent, I found lots of information on social media.

The Garones had been married for more than ten years. Neither had a previous marriage. It appeared unlikely Gina had been affected by Maureen in the latter's capacity as a divorce attorney. And Carolyn Whitcome specifically told me that Gina's animosity toward Maureen only started two months ago.

What happened at that time?

My second internet search was for Sam Garcia. He was single. I discovered his family's restaurant, El Mar, had been an expensive five-star dining establishment located on Randall Street in the Village of Scallop Bay Cove. An old restaurant review claimed it was well worth the long wait to secure a reservation. El Mar closed more than two years ago.

I also found an obituary for Sam's father, Oscar Garcia. He died less than one year ago, but no cause of death was listed. Was I wrong in thinking Sam lied? Maybe the restaurant did close because of his father's health.

But it didn't matter. Nothing connected Sam to Maureen.

Next, I looked into Lee Adler. On a whim, I decided to see if I could discover anything about his father's jewelry business. I had no idea of the store's name, so I typed Adler Jewelry into the search engine and hoped for the best.

Adler and Link Jewelry Shoppe came up. I was taken aback at what I saw.

His father's jewelry company went out of business because of tax fraud. Lee's parents were never charged—they appeared to be victims too. But the firm's other partner, Daniel Link, was charged and convicted. The business had to pay back taxes and substantial fines, which bankrupted the company.

"But Maureen was a divorce lawyer, not a tax attorney," I mumbled to myself as I told myself there's no connection here.

Or is there? I wondered.

Lee hadn't told me the entire story. But was that simply because he was embarrassed? Before I could consider this further, my phone trilled. Abby's name popped up,

I asked my daughter to join me at my meeting in Manhattan later this afternoon with Teresa Lamonica. I explained the pretense of the meeting and what I hoped to learn.

"Do I have a purpose at this meeting other than keeping you company?" she asked after agreeing to attend.

"I'll need you to act as a representative of your father's veterinary practice. I know he's volunteering at the spay and neuter clinic today and wouldn't make it into the city on time."

Abby laughed. "I don't think he would come even if he was available. I'm surprised he agreed to attend the Ajax Pet Products dinner and sales meeting on Sunday. I know how he feels about your investigating or as he refers to it—satisfying your insatiable curiosity."

"You're being kind. He usually refers to it as snooping."

Abby and I started discussing the murder investigation. I told her I wasn't having much luck.

"I'm researching background on the sanctuary staff, but aside from Nick Lamonica, I haven't found anyone else connected to Maureen."

"What's your next step?" she asked.

"Maureen's wake is Saturday. I plan on attending and talking to those present. Social media is helpful, but I've always found the best way to uncover truths is by talking."

After we said good-bye, I fished inside my tote bag and pulled out the notes I'd taken at the sanctuary. When I finished organizing them, I realized I hadn't heard back from Detective Fox, so I decided to be a pest and call again. I was just about to punch in his number when my phone trilled. The readout on the screen told me it was Detective Fox.

"I was about to call you," I said after I pushed the button to accept the call and raised the phone to my ear.

"Have you checked the security tapes at the front gate?" I asked before he had a chance to say anything. "Do you know who entered the sanctuary the morning Maureen's body was found?" I wanted to be sure I wasn't missing anyone.

"Besides Maureen, only Gina Garone, Nick Lamonica, Sam Garcia, Lee Adler, and Declan Carr," he said, confirming the names I had on my list. "Oh, you were on the list too, but I'm excluding you as a suspect. Wolfe's excluding you too, although if he could, he would love to make you suspect number one." I could hear Fox chuckle.

"I believe the sanctuary has one other full time animal keeper," I said. I had seen the position and salary when I looked over the budget. "I'm assuming that person was not there on the morning of the murder."

"Right. That full-time keeper is on vacation for two weeks. And no volunteers were at the sanctuary at that time either. They all come in much later in the day."

"Have you checked alibis of those present?" I asked.

"Nick and Sam were together—but only for ten minutes."

"Both Gina and Lee left their offices unexpectedly that morning," I said.

"They told me where they were, but no one saw them." He sighed. "No one has a verifiable alibi for the entire time."

I still wondered why Lee canceled our appointment, and why Gina rushed away from the office so abruptly.

"Wolfe has a person of interest." Fox said, before I had a chance to question him as to the whereabouts of Lee and Gina. "It's the reason I'm calling you."

I had a bad feeling. I sucked in my breath.

"Declan Carr," he said.

"I've known Declan for years. He's not a murderer. He's an old friend of Abby."

"Unfortunately, murderers sometimes have friends."

"Why is he focused on Declan?"

Declan has motive—"

"So does Nick Lamonica," I argued. I told him how Maureen was once a divorce attorney and that Nick's ex-wife had been a client.

"I didn't know that. Wolfe didn't dig that deep."

Of course, he didn't.

"I promise I'll look into the background of all five suspects," Fox added, "but there is evidence pointing to Declan Carr."

"What type of evidence?"

"Maureen was killed by an injection of an animal sedative."

"That's still circumstantial. Someone else may have gotten hold of it." I didn't tell Fox I knew about the etorphine.

Then the detective told me something I didn't know.

"He also threatened Maureen," Fox said. "Nick and Sam heard him arguing with her a few days before her murder."

"You don't kill someone because you're arguing."

"It was more than an argument. His exact words were, 'We would all be better off if you were dead'."

CHAPTER 17

"What do you hope to discover?" Abby asked once we were seated in the fourteenth-floor lounge of the Bancroft Hotel in Manhattan, waiting for Nick Lamonica's ex-wife.

"I'm not sure. But the more information we can gather on pet supplies, the better equipped we'll be to scrutinize the Ajax company."

"I'm skeptical. I think—"

"Oh, here comes Teresa now," I interrupted. "I recognize her from the description she gave on the phone."

I stood up and motioned Teresa Lamonica to our table, which was next to a floor to ceiling window overlooking Central Park. Teresa had wide green eyes and a dazzling smile. She slipped into a chair, and we introduced ourselves.

The server approached. It was five-thirty, so I ordered my favorite, a pomegranate martini, while Abby and Teresa opted for white wine.

"We have a wide range of grooming supplies, and we've recently added pet toys," Teresa said, getting straight to the point. She pulled up her company's website on her iPad. "I find that toys are big sellers in veterinary clinics."

Abby nodded and grinned. "Dogs and cats stress out at the vet's office. I can see clients treating their furry friends to toys as a reward after a medical exam or procedure."

As Teresa scrolled down, Abby scanned the screen, occasionally asking a question.

"Do we order the products directly online?"

Teresa shook her head, causing her shoulder length chestnut hair to slide from side to side. "Not if you want the group discount. The online catalog prices are for pet parents who only order a few items. If you're ordering in bulk, you need to deal with a sales representative like me."

As the server delivered our drinks, Teresa fished into her bag and pulled out a discounted price list which she handed to my daughter. "Find what you want on our website, and then call me. Nothing is set in stone. I can negotiate the prices on this list too. The larger the order, the larger the discount."

Teresa went on to push several of the products in the catalog. She struck me as a woman who didn't take no for an answer.

"Thanks," Abby said. "I'll discuss this with my father, and we'll get back to you."

Abby shot me a look. I smiled weakly. Matt might order a few products for his own use in the veterinary hospital, but he had no intention of selling merchandise. I hated wasting Teresa's time, but this was the only guise I could use to meet her. There was another topic I needed to discuss, so I changed the subject of our conversation.

"Have you heard of Ajax Pet Products?" I asked.

Teresa furrowed her brows and shook her head. "No. It's not one of our major competitors. Is it a new company?"

"I don't know. But it's a franchise." I realized if Teresa hadn't heard of Ajax, the company was operating under the radar.

Teresa scowled. "Before you make a purchasing decision, please keep in mind that Omega has been around for more than fifty years. Our products are of top value as is our service. Be careful of dealing with what could be a fly-by-night operation."

"My husband has no intention of dealing with Ajax." I was now ready to segue into a different topic. "I'm so glad your husband recommended you."

"Ex-husband." Teresa smiled.

I smiled back. "It's great when ex-spouses have good relationships."

"Well, it's better now."

"It wasn't always friendly?" I asked.

"No. I hired an attorney who fought for the best deal for me. I can't help it if Nick hired the brother-in-law of a friend who was only three years out of law school. This guy didn't specialize in divorce. He was a jack of all trades—wills, real estate closings, contracts. This was only his second divorce case. My attorney handled only divorces."

"So, you made out better than Nick?"

"Yes. I have the children, and I want the best for them. My attorney got them enough money, so I could send them to private school. They go to Ellis Academy."

I'd heard of Ellis Academy since it was located only a few blocks away from where my old college roommate lived in southern California. It was a prestigious and super expensive boarding school.

"In the beginning, Nick complained about how little money he had left after paying child support. But money had never been important to him before this." Teresa began sounding a bit defensive. "He was happy working with his animals and living simply."

But he probably enjoyed eating regular meals and having a roof over his head. I didn't voice this thought.

"We've been divorced seven years. Once his aunt died three years ago, he inherited a little money, and things got better. Before that he was especially angry that he couldn't see the kids. He couldn't afford to travel across the country to visit them."

"What about summer vacations? Didn't he see them then?"

Teresa sipped her wine before answering. "When they were younger, they attended sleep-away camps also run by Ellis Academy. My daughter went to one that specialized in dance and my son a music camp. Between their time at school and summer camp, the kids rarely got to visit with their father."

She shrugged. "He should have managed his money more carefully or gotten a job that paid more."

Teresa's phone beeped a text message. She glanced down at it. "I better get going." She sipped a bit more wine, leaving the glass half full.

"Get back to me on what products you want," she said to Abby while motioning the server for a check. "I'll take care of the bill."

Abby and I remained at the table after she left.

"What do you think?" Abby asked.

"Nick told me his kids are now fifteen and sixteen, which means they were eight and nine at the time of the divorce. He didn't get the money from his aunt's estate until three years ago."

"That meant for more than four years he had almost no contact with his children."

I sipped my pomegranate martini before speaking. "Eating spaghetti with ketchup, giving up your car, and moving into a boarding house are one thing. But not being able to see your children…" I shook my head. "That would make me want to kill someone."

CHAPTER 18

"I'm not buying a franchise. It's—"

"I know," I interrupted. "But play along. We need to find out more about Ajax Pet Products."

It was Friday night. Matt and I were on our way to Marcia Silver's home. My mother had been there, visiting with her friend since late afternoon.

"Here we are," I said as we pulled in front of Marcia's small ranch house which featured a gorgeous garden in the front. It had rained earlier, and the fragrance of roses and wet grass wafted through the evening breeze.

Marcia and my mother had no sooner greeted us when Abby and Jason arrived. Since Marcia knew my daughter but never met Jason, I introduced him.

"He's one of the only people I know who is as tall as Matt," my mother added. Jason was a former college football quarterback.

"I've heard so much about you," Marcia gushed. "Assistant District Attorney—that's impressive."

Jason's smile faded, and he frowned but only for a moment. He quickly smiled again and greeted his hostess.

But I wondered what caused the frown.

"Does everyone want coffee?" Marcia asked. "I made brownies too."

Marcia was a petite woman in her early seventies. But unlike my mother, she wasn't a youthful looking seventy. With her wrinkled skin and short gray hair, she appeared every bit her age.

"Regular or decaffeinated?" she asked.

I picked regular. No way was I a decaffeinated type of person. Everyone else chose to go caffeine free.

Moments later, we were settled in her small living room with our coffee and brownies. As we engaged in preliminary small talk, I wondered how much money Marcia had invested. I remembered my mother had been worried when Marcia bought the condo in Florida.

"I don't know if she can afford the upkeep," my mother had said to me at the time. "If the condo board raises the assessment, Marcia is in big trouble. She'll go through her savings in no time."

I didn't know what would happen if Marcia lost money in a pyramid scam.

I was jolted out of my thoughts as I heard Abby say to Marcia, "Why don't you tell us a bit about Ajax Pet Products. I think my dad has some questions."

I was sitting on the couch next to Matt in case I needed to give him a gentle nudge.

Turns out, I did.

"Ask her now," I whispered to my husband, who was discussing with Jason whether brownies were better with or without nuts.

"I'd like to see some of the merchandise from your company, Marcia," Matt said. "Do you have anything here?"

"No, but I have a catalog." She paused. "That's if I can find it. I haven't used it in a while. I'm not into selling the merchandise. My sales manager says to push the franchises."

I frowned. One of the major components of a pyramid scam was that there was no emphasis on product—only on franchises.

"I'd still like to see the catalog," Matt said "Have you sold any products?

"A few. My sales totaled about one hundred fifty dollars."

"If you don't mind my asking, how much commission did you make?" I asked.

Marcia stared at her shoes. "Ten percent. Fifteen dollars. Most sales were to your mother."

"The merchandise is expensive, and a lot is out of stock," my mother added.

"Let me see if I can find the catalog for you, Matt. I'll check my bedroom."

"I ordered a nail clipper for Merlin," my mother said as Marcia took off in search of her catalog. It hasn't arrived yet, but as soon as it does, I'll give it to you, Kristy. I was hoping to have it by now. Merlin needs it."

I didn't tell her Matt owned several clippers. Most cat owners did not want to clip their feline's nails and preferred to have a veterinarian or groomer do it.

"How long ago did you order the clippers?" I asked.

"Seven weeks ago."

"Did you know it would take that long?"

"No. The catalog said most items delivered in two weeks."

"But if there's a big demand, delivery can be delayed." Marcia returned with the catalog, which turned out to be three sheets of paper stapled together. "You did get the dog shampoo on time, didn't you, Mary?"

My mother nodded and turned to face me. "That's the shampoo I gave you for Brandy and Archie."

"I haven't used it yet, but I will soon," I promised.

Marcia handed Matt the so-called catalog. Abby rose from her chair and stood behind the sofa. She and I both looked over Matt's shoulder as he scanned each of the three pages. Products were listed along with their descriptions, but there were no pictures.

My daughter, pointing to a listing of a cream for hot spots on dogs, whispered. "Look at that item. It's nearly twice as much as the one in the Omega online catalog, the one that Nick Lamonica's ex-wife showed us."

"I wonder if it's that much better," I mumbled to my daughter.

"I wonder if it is better at all." Abby frowned.

As we quickly glanced at the items for sale, Abby pointed to several other products selling for a significantly higher amount than those offered by Omega Animal Grooming Supplies.

"Is there a website too?" I asked.

"No. Our regional sales manager says Ajax is an old-fashioned company—one that believes in a personal approach not a digital one."

"How did you get started with the pyra—er—investment?" I was curious how investors were recruited.

"My friend Betty saw an advertisement posted on a bulletin board in her senior center. It offered a free dinner at Alfredo's restaurant if you came and listened to a talk on how to become rich." Marcia smiled. "Free dinner. Become rich. That's a win-win."

Jason remained silent, but he appeared to be taking in every word that was said. He also appeared to be enjoying his third brownie.

"What went on at the dinner?" Abby asked.

"There were a few testimonies from other investors who talked about how successful they had become. Betty thought the opportunity sounded almost too good to be true, so she bought a franchise. Around two months ago, she invited me to their monthly dinner and sales meeting. I attended and purchased a franchise through her."

"How much did you pay for the franchise?"

She hesitated, looked around the room, and finally said.

"Franchises cost eight thousand."

Matt let out a low whistle. It was a substantial amount to lose, but it was also below the ten-thousand-dollar mark that often puts internal revenue and bank officials on alert. Whoever ran this scam was a smart cookie.

"When Betty sold a franchise to me, she made ten percent of the sale price. That's eight hundred dollars," Marcia added.

"How many more franchises has Betty sold?"

Marcia's face clouded. "None. Mine was the only one."

"So she made eight hundred dollars back of her eight thousand investment. Did Betty sell any products?"

"Not really. I think she bought a toy for her poodle."

I stayed silent while sipping my coffee. Silence was often the best way to keep people talking.

It worked. Marcia continued, "Austin Wells, the company's regional sales manager, said the first few months could be difficult. But once the investor got the hang of selling, it would take off. He assured me that after a few months most investors have recouped their investment, and everything after that is pure profit."

"Have you sold any franchises?"

Marcia shook her head. "Hopefully, Matt will be my first." She faced my husband, "So Matt, are you in?"

"I'm sorry, Marcia," Matt said. "But it doesn't look—"

Abby interrupted, "Why don't you go to the sales meeting this Sunday, Dad? Why don't we all go?"

"If nothing else, you'll get a free dinner," Marcia added.

I gently nudged Matt, and he agreed to attend. Abby and I also said we'd go.

"I'll text the regional sales manager now and make reservations," Marcia said as she pulled out her phone. "Jason, are you coming too?"

"Unfortunately, I can't attend. I've tickets for this Sunday's

Yankees game. I'm taking my nephew for his birthday."

No. I was sure he did not have Yankees tickets. Matt, Abby, and I were avid Yankees fans, but Jason was one hundred percent for the Mets. So was his nephew. Why would they go to a Yankee game?

I was taken aback, but then it dawned on me what he was doing. It was also the reason he frowned earlier when Marcia said she was aware that he was an assistant district attorney.

Jason realized the damage that could be done if Marcia mentioned his occupation to Austin Wells, the regional sales manager. The last thing a scammer needed was a law enforcement person in the midst. Any chance we had of gathering incriminating evidence would be gone. Jason wasn't going to a ball game—this was the first excuse he could think of that fast.

Abby, Matt, and I would need to handle the meeting.

"Your mother's attitude changed," Matt said as we drove home. "She was a bit critical of the company tonight. She mentioned the merchandise was expensive and frequently out of stock. Do you think she knows now that Ajax Pet Products is a scam?"

"My mother is stubborn, but she's also smart. She's been spending a lot of time with Marcia. I'll bet she realizes something is up."

Before I could say any more, my phone trilled.

"It's Detective Fox," I said. "It's also eleven o'clock at night. What could he want at this hour?"

"There's only one way to find out," Matt said. "Answer it."

CHAPTER 19

"Your friend got a reprieve," Detective Fox said once I answered. "As of now, we're not arresting Declan Carr."

"What changed?"

"The brass wants to be careful and not rush into anything. Wolfe made serious mistakes in a few previous homicides. He arrested suspects prematurely who were later found to be innocent."

"This is great news about Declan—"

"It's not that great," Fox interrupted. "This is only a postponement. In all likelihood, unless there's a break in the case, Declan will eventually be arrested."

Before I could speak, Fox continued. "Wolfe feels we have the big three: motive, means, and opportunity. The accusation Maureen filed against Declan is the motive. Means is etorphine—"

"What about opportunity?" I asked. "All the suspects had the same opportunity."

"All the others followed their daily routine. But not Declan. We were told Declan always checks the animals in the veterinary infirmary around seven—when he first arrives. The day of the murder, Lee Adler stopped by the infirmary at seven-fifteen, and Declan wasn't there.

"Why did Lee stop by?"

"I don't know. Wolfe didn't ask."

Lee had postponed his interview with me that morning. I wondered what was so important that he had to see Declan.

"The point is Declan wasn't at the infirmary," Fox said. "He should have been."

This was not good news. "Did you ask him where he was?"

"He claimed he spotted a deer in distress on his way to the infirmary. The deer's head was caught in an opening in a fence. The fence had been erected to enclose a small area upfront where new grass seed had been planted. Declan released the deer and waited about thirty minutes to make sure the animal was okay. He said he used that time to block the hole in the fence, so the animal wouldn't get caught again."

"Don't you believe him?"

"No witnesses. No proof"

"There's still no hard evidence," I argued.

"I know. That's why the brass wants to be sure due diligence is done before making an arrest."

Due diligence from Detective Wolfe was highly unlikely. Still, I was grateful for the extra time.

But I knew I'd need to race the clock to find the killer before Wolfe put the handcuffs on Declan Carr.

CHAPTER 20

"I didn't expect this place to be so empty," I whispered to my daughter.

Abby and I had arrived at the funeral parlor for Maureen McDermott's wake on Saturday, about an hour after it started. The wake was a short one—only one day, between two and four in the afternoon.

I took a moment to survey my surroundings. There were no photos of the deceased and no flowers. Only five other people were in the room. A man, woman, and teenage boy were mulling about in the back. Two females, dressed in dark clothes, stood upfront near the closed casket. One appeared to be in her late forties, the other in her late teens. Both women resembled Maureen with their fair skin, blue eyes, and dark hair.

I assumed the women had a connection to the deceased, so I approached them.

"I'm Kristy Farrell, and this is my daughter Abby," I said. "I knew Maureen from the animal sanctuary."

"I'm Nora. Maureen's sister. This is Erin, my daughter," the older woman said. "Thank you for coming. I don't expect many of her co-workers to show."

I hadn't said I was a co-worker, but if that was what she assumed, it was all for the better. She might clam up if she knew I was a reporter.

"Perhaps others will show up later," I responded.

"I doubt it. My sister always had a problem with co-workers. She had a problem with people in general."

Nora paused and stared at the casket before turning her attention back to me. "The sanctuary director—I think she said her name was Gina—she showed up here at exactly two o'clock and left after five minutes. She probably thought a visit was expected of her since she was Maureen's boss."

"She also said it was busy season at the sanctuary, so most of the staff wouldn't be coming," Erin added with a smirk. "I didn't think the sanctuary had a busy season."

"Sounds like a polite excuse." I didn't know what else to say. We all stood silently for an awkward moment.

"Those three are Maureen's neighbors. They're from way down the block," Erin said, breaking the silence. She pointed to the trio in the back of the room.

"But her adjacent neighbors aren't here." Nora poured water into a glass from a nearby pitcher, took a sip, and continued. "When I called to tell them about the funeral arrangements, the one who lives in the house on her left hung up on me. The neighbor to her right flat out said no. He wouldn't come. Maureen had reported him a year ago for a minor zoning violation."

"But those three in the back came."

"Yes. Maureen rescued Max, their dog. He had escaped from their yard, and Maureen helped with the search. She was the one who found Max."

I had a feeling if animals were allowed at funerals, this place might be full.

"Did you get along with your sister?" I asked.

"Not really. There's a ten-year age difference. I think she resented me from the moment I was born."

"My mother tried to be friends," Erin piped in. "She even

asked Aunt Maureen to be my godmother."

Nora shook her head. "Maureen declined. She said the only reason I asked her was so she'd send better gifts. That was the furthest thing from my mind."

"Mom always invited Aunt Maureen to our house for the holidays. Sometimes she came, but most times she didn't. Do you know she never sent me a birthday card? My dad refused to come today. I didn't want to be here either, but Mom felt it was the right thing to do."

"I felt it was time to put Maureen's petty actions behind us."

"Petty actions! I don't think what she did when I needed that operation can be called petty." Erin's face turned the color of a beet. "Why don't you tell these people what happened?"

Nora sighed audibly. "When Erin was three years old, she needed surgery. I had insurance, but it was the type where I had to pay upfront and then get reimbursed from the insurance company. I didn't have that kind of money to lay out, and the hospital wouldn't operate unless I paid in full. I asked Maureen if she could lend me some money, knowing I'd be able to pay her back later that year. She said no. I had to get a loan."

"Is it possible she couldn't afford—"

"She had plenty of money. She was cheap and mean spirited. But she's my only relative, besides Erin and my husband. I figured I needed to arrange a funeral and be here for a final good-bye."

Erin glanced at the door. "This is going to be a long afternoon."

"What about her colleagues from when she worked as a lawyer" I asked. "Do you think they might show?"

"And her clients?" added Abby.

A wiry smile appeared on Nora's face. "Clients, maybe. Some might come. She worked hard and got top dollar for them. If she wanted, she could be…" Nora paused, smiled, and said, "*almost* charming."

"But her colleagues despised her," Erin said. "Even Joyce isn't coming, and she worked with Aunt Maureen for more than twenty years."

"Joyce was Maureen's administrative assistant," Nora explained. "When I called Joyce, she simply said she couldn't make it. Didn't give a reason."

"I take it they didn't like each other."

"Joyce ran the office, including handling all the scheduling. Maureen was always a difficult boss. But the final straw was when Maureen decided to give up her law practice and go back to school to prepare for a career with animals. She never told anyone. Maureen knew months in advance when classes would start, but she only gave Joyce one week's notice on closing the law practice."

"They spent that final week notifying clients, referring cases, and ironing out loose ends," Erin added, shaking her head. "After that, Joyce received one week's severance pay—after two decades of service."

"It was worse than that." Nora said. "Joyce asked for a job recommendation. Maureen told her she didn't have time to write one. She'd get to it in a month or two. Who would hire someone without a recommendation from your boss, especially when you worked for the same person for twenty years—"

"She also told Joyce not to have any prospective employer call for at least six weeks," Erin interrupted. "My aunt said she'd be too busy to answer questions."

An idea popped into my mind.

"I think Maureen mentioned Joyce once," I lied. "Joyce Anderson, right?" I felt my nose growing.

"No. Not even close," Nora responded. "Joyce Miller."

"Right. Maybe I got the name confused with someone else," I lied again. "Doesn't Joyce live in Levittown?" My nose was really growing.

"No. Wantagh. You really must have her mixed up with someone else."

Abby stared at me with a puzzled expression across her face.

I was about to say good-bye when Erin asked, "What type of work do you do at the sanctuary?"

"I don't work for the sanctuary," I confessed, deciding to come clean. "I'm a reporter for *Animal Advocate Magazine,* and I'm writing a story about the place."

"About Aunt Maureen's murder?"

"The story is about the sanctuary and the rescued animals, but, yes, I will probably include a segment on the murder."

"I'm aware the police think the killer is a member of the staff," Nora stated in a matter of fact manner. "What do you think?"

"I'm afraid I agree. Her co-workers are the only ones who had access to the murder site."

"I would think you really have to hate someone to kill them," Erin said. "I guess Aunt Maureen did more than just irritate her co-workers."

We stood silently. I realized Nora and Erin were good sources of information as to Maureen's past. I couldn't think of any questions to ask right now, but something would surely come up in the future. I needed to be able to contact these two women.

"I'd like to exchange phone numbers?" I said.

"Sure, but why?"

"If I discover something new, I may want to talk with you."

"But we don't know anything."

"You may know more than you realize." I fished into my bag, pulled out two business cards, and handed them to Nora and Erin. They provided me with their phone numbers in exchange.

As my daughter and I departed, Abby's expression was one of puzzlement again.

"What was with those questions you asked earlier about

Maureen's former administrative assistant, Joyce? You don't really know her, do you?"

"Of course not. But I need to talk to this woman. I was afraid if I asked Nora or Erin for Joyce's contact information they might refuse. So I pretended we were acquainted, and I tried to find out more about her. It worked. I have the name and the community where she lives. Now, I should be able to find her."

"But why do you want to contact her?

"Because, as an administrative assistant to Maureen, especially one who handled the scheduling, Joyce should be a treasure trove of information."

CHAPTER 21

After church Sunday morning, I searched on my laptop, and found the address of Maureen's administrative assistant, Joyce Miller. It was only twenty minutes away from where I lived, so I decided to drive to her house. Since it was a rainy day, I hoped there was a good chance I'd catch her at home.

In researching Joyce on social media, I discovered she was involved in an innocence project that investigated old court cases where a person may have been wrongly convicted. If she felt that strongly about justice, I had a feeling she would try to be helpful in my quest to find Maureen McDermott's killer.

The woman who answered the door at Joyce's Cape Cod home was tall and thin with dark brown hair pulled back into a ponytail. She wore sweats and was holding a bottle of vitamin water.

I introduced myself and explained why I was here.

"I'm Joyce. Please come in. I was about to go on my treadmill, but that can wait. I'm glad to help you, but I don't know how."

"I only have a few questions."

"Can I offer you vitamin water, a fruit smoothie, or herbal tea?" she asked as she led me into the kitchen.

I would have loved a coffee, but that didn't appear to be an option. I declined her drink offer.

"I imagine Maureen was difficult to work for," I said, once

settled on a high stool by her breakfast bar.

Joyce nodded. "Anyone who got in her way—watch out. Maureen was vengeful and went for the jugular. But in the beginning, she wasn't too bad with me. She could be demanding and sarcastic, but the money was good. And when she married, she actually became nicer."

Joyce's face clouded. "Once her husband died, she became a horror. Even if she hadn't closed the office, I was getting ready to quit."

"Do you recognize any of these names?" I asked. I handed her a sheet of paper where I'd written the following:

Nick Lamonica

Gina Garone

Lee Adler

Declan Carr

Sam Garcia

"Nick Lamonica. Boy! Did he get a rough deal," Joyce said as she examined the list. "I never heard of Gina Garone. Lee Adler doesn't sound familiar either. I don't know a Declan Carr, but Maureen did deal with a Regina Carr, who was an attorney. If I remember correctly, Regina was active in the bar association."

I jotted that down on my note pad. Carr was a common name, but it was possible that Regina was related to Declan.

"Same thing with Sam Garcia. I don't know him, but I recall an Oscar Garcia. He owned an upscale restaurant called El Mar, and Maureen was responsible for its going out of business."

"Was the restaurant part of a divorce settlement?" I asked.

Joyce shook her head. "No. Maureen went there for dinner with another lawyer—a big shot in the bar association whom she was trying to impress. The restaurant messed up her reservation and couldn't accommodate them. Maureen was embarrassed and furious. And when Maureen was furious, she would seek revenge."

"So how did she close the restaurant?"

"A few weeks after the incident, Maureen secured a lunch reservation at the place. It was only a five-minute drive from our office. On the day of her reservation, right before she left for the restaurant, Maureen called a former client who was a top administrator for the health department. Maureen had helped this client get a huge divorce settlement."

Joyce sipped her water and continued. "Anyway, she asked this former client if she could send a health inspector to the restaurant, claiming it was infested with roaches."

"Was that true?" I asked. According to everything I read about El Mar, it was an outstanding restaurant. I was aware the appearance of a restaurant's dining room sometimes bore no relationship to the condition of its kitchen. But still, if it were "infested with roaches," several of these creatures would have found their way into the public eating area, and that information would have been posted online immediately.

"It wasn't true until a few minutes after making the call, Maureen strolled into the restaurant for her reservation and let some loose." Joyce shook her head. "Not long after that, a health department inspector showed up. I heard a customer saw a roach and shrieked just as the inspector entered."

For a moment, I was speechless.

"Maureen told you she did this?" I finally asked.

"No, but it is true." Joyce smiled. "I heard her on the phone asking for the inspection."

"She may have assumed almost any restaurant would have some violations. That in itself—"

Joyce held up her hand. "I also saw a copy of Maureen's email confirmation order for roaches. She left it on her desk." Joyce paused. "You can get anything online."

Now that was incriminating.

"Did anyone else know what she did?" I asked.

"I'm pretty sure Oscar Garcia found out. He was a hands-on owner and would be aware if there really were roaches. He had to assume someone planted them."

"Yes. But that doesn't mean it was Maureen."

"He dealt with the health inspectors for more than two decades." Joyce smiled knowingly. "He probably had a contact in the department who told him."

"Probably?" I asked.

"I'm sure he did. Two days after the incident, I overheard Maureen on the phone with her health administrator friend. Maureen said 'so what if he knows the complaint came from me. It turned out to be true, didn't it?'"

I digested what Joyce told me. Oscar knew the roaches were planted. Since he most likely discovered the complaint came from Maureen, who was furious with him and had come to the restaurant that day, he had to assume she put them there.

No doubt Oscar told his son.

I now had a motive for Sam Garcia.

CHAPTER 22

"I hope dinner is yummy," Abby said. "I'm starving."

I rolled my eyes. My daughter, a size six, ate like a longshoreman. Luckily, she exercised like an Olympic contender.

Abby, Matt, and I pulled into the parking lot of the Owl's Nest Inn for the Ajax Pet Products monthly dinner and sales meeting. Marcia had told us the dinners were at different restaurants each month.

This restaurant, with its knotty pine walls and subdued lighting, created a cozy atmosphere. We were directed to the backroom where a dozen round tables surrounded a long buffet table that ran through the middle. In the front was a dais with two chairs.

My mother and Marcia Silver had driven here earlier and now sat at one of the round tables. They waved us over.

"We saved these seats for you," Marcia said. She introduced us to three people also sitting at the table. "This is Gustav, Jack, and Jill."

Gustav was an elderly gentleman with wild hair that made him look a bit like Rasputin. Jack and Jill—whose names made me chuckle—were newlyweds who appeared to be in their late twenties.

An announcement was made. "The buffet is now open."

We all bee-lined for the food table, except for Gustav. He

made his way to the bar with his almost empty glass. Drinks were free. I'm sure the purpose was to pump the potential clients with liquor, so they would be more receptive to making a deal.

"Someone likes garlic," Marcia said, once we were back with our plates loaded with food. She wrinkled her nose as if garlic was not a favorable aroma. It was to me.

"I'm the guilty one," I said, looking down at my heaping of linguini with clam sauce, salad with Italian dressing, and a big slab of garlic bread.

"So, how did you get involved with Ajax Pet Products?" I asked my tablemates before I started eating.

"I'm a graduate student, and I only work part-time," answered Jack. "Jill is looking for a teaching job, but right now she's working as a teacher's assistant. We're finding it hard to make ends meet. When this opportunity came up, it was the perfect solution."

"How could you afford to invest?" Abby asked.

"We invested some of the money we received at our wedding," Jill said. "We originally planned to use our wedding cash to supplement our income while Jack's in school, but we decided to take part of the money and buy a franchise."

"We'll make a lot more selling franchises then just having the money sit in a bank," Jack added.

I winced. "How have you been doing so far?"

Jack frowned. Jill's face clouded.

"Not too well," Jill said. "But we've only been at it two months."

I noted my mother was unusually quiet.

"Have you sold any franchises yet?" I asked the young couple.

Jill shook her head. "Most of our friends are in school or paying back student loans. They don't have discretionary funds."

Jack smiled. "But I think we'll be okay. Our next step is to approach family. My aunt's birthday party is next week, and I'll propose this opportunity to my cousins."

"I hope you have better luck than me," added Gustav. He swallowed part of his drink, which from the color and odor appeared to be scotch. "I've hit up every relative, but only sold one to my nephew."

"You'll sell," Marcia said. "You need patience and perseverance."

He shook his head. "I'm starting to become discouraged. I don't—"

"How's everyone doing?" A man, lanky in build with red hair worn crew cut style, approached our table. He was baby faced with full cheeks and big blue eyes exuding a boyish charm. His age was hard to judge, but I would guess he was in his forties.

"Austin, this is Matt Farrell, the veterinarian I was telling you about." Marcia said, pointing to my husband. "He's thinking about investing." She then said, "Matt, this is Austin Wells, the regional sales manager for Ajax."

Austin grinned. His smile was warm, but there was a glint in his eyes that made me wary.

"Great to meet you, Matt." He reached over and pumped Matt's arm. "Let's talk right after the program. Hope you'll join the Ajax family."

Austin put his hand on Gustav's shoulder. "I heard what you said. Don't get discouraged. I want you to listen carefully to our speaker. What she has to say will definitely encourage you."

Gustav took another swig of his drink, and Austin took off. Before I knew, Austin was behind the dais. He grabbed the microphone and called for the crowd's attention.

"Thank you for coming tonight. Rather than listen to me, I want you to hear from one of our success stories."

He sipped his water. "I'd like to introduce a lady who in one year has sold twenty franchises, doubling—that's right, doubling—her investment. And many of her investors sold franchises too. You know what that means. Commissions! Please give a warm welcome to Millie Topper."

The woman seated on his right rose to a round of applause. She appeared to be about forty with buttery blond hair and a little too much make-up for my liking. While the audience was clapping, I grabbed my phone and discretely shot photos of Austin and Millie.

"Thank you," Millie said once the applause subsided. "I want to tell everyone who has invested in Ajax Pet Products, as well as those who plan to invest tonight, that you are on your way to success. Never get discouraged. I didn't sell anything at first. Then all of a sudden, it popped."

She paused for more applause and went on. "I joined an exercise class at my community center, and I sold to four people. A few days later, I went to an anniversary party and sold another three. From that point, it blossomed."

"She's a shill," Abby whispered to me. "Bet she's connected to Austin."

I nodded. "Her purpose is to lead the audience on."

To my surprise, my mother nodded and quietly said, "I thought this was a great opportunity for Marcia and for Matt too. But the more I see, the less I like it. Matt shouldn't invest, but poor Marcia."

My mother finally saw the light.

After Millie's speech, Austin talked for a few minutes and ended the program. He soon made his way to our table.

"Are you ready to become part of the Ajax family and make a fortune?" he asked Matt.

"I'm ready to talk," Matt answered, glancing at me.

"Let's go to the bar," Austin suggested. "I have a few other interested investors waiting for us there."

"You've got to stall," I whispered to my husband. "When he asks you to buy a franchise, don't say no. Tell him you're interested, but make up an excuse why you can't invest tonight. I need more time to investigate."

Matt winked and went off to the bar. Forty minutes later, he returned to our table.

"Austin wanted me to sign up now, but I told him it would need to wait." Matt grinned. "I lied that we were leaving tomorrow for a vacation in Montauk, and I'd invest when I return."

"How did he take that?" I asked, remembering the ABCs of sales—Always Be Closing."

"He wasn't at all happy, but he reluctantly agreed. He had no choice. He's coming to our house a week from this Wednesday."

"Does that give you enough time to investigate, Mom?" Abby asked.

"I hope so."

"Good. It's all settled. Let's get dessert," Matt suggested.

The buffet table now featured coffee and tea as well as several trays of cookies. While Matt and I went up to get our caffeine and sugar fix, Abby headed to the rest room.

"I didn't expect you to be such a willing participant tonight," I said with a grin. "You don't normally like my involvement in this sort of thing."

"Do you mean criminal cases?" He grinned back. "You're right. But I don't think this one puts you in physical danger. And those poor people who invested..." He shook his head. "They need help."

"Were any other marks meeting with Austin at the bar?" I asked, getting back to what just transpired.

"Two others. One bought on the spot. The other said he had to discuss with his wife. Austin is meeting with them this Thursday."

"Did you find out anything about the actual products?

Matt poured coffee for me and a cup for him. "Austin evaded questions about the merchandise, but he eventually slipped and mentioned a factory upstate, but I've no idea where."

"That covers a lot of territory. I'll do a computer search tomorrow and see if I can narrow it down, although I haven't found out anything about the company so far."

Abby returned from the rest room and joined us at the dessert table. Her face expressed worry. "Do you think Austin will follow through and meet up with you?"

"Yes, I do." Matt frowned. "Why do you ask? Do you think there's a problem?"

"I'm not sure. As I was returning, I saw Austin and Mille alone at the bar. I decided to snoop, so I moved closer. Their backs were to me. Austin said several investors were starting to complain. He said it was time to leave Long Island."

CHAPTER 23

I wasn't having any luck.

Although I'm not a morning person, I was up early trying to find out where the Ajax Pet Products factory was located, but there was nothing on the internet. Marcia Silver had mentioned they didn't have a website, but it appeared that Ajax had no digital presence at all.

The two dogs padded into the kitchen where I was working. Archie rested his huge head on my foot, while Brandy placed her chin on my lap. Soon after, Merlin paraded in, trailed by my mother. The cat hopped on the windowsill, while my mother made her way to the coffee maker.

"You came home late last night," I said. "Did you and Marcia go somewhere?"

"No. We both had our own cars. She went home." My mother poured coffee and slid into a chair, a Cheshire cat grin on her face.

"What did you do?" I knew she was dying for me to ask.

"I decided to follow Austin Wells—"

"Mom! That was dangerous." I jumped up, toppling the dogs.

"Not at all." She waved her hand dismissively and continued grinning. "And it was well worth it."

I slumped back down in my chair. Brandy wandered off, but Archie, the canine tank, rested his head back on my foot.

"What did you discover?" I asked.

"He's staying at the Parkside Hotel."

I nodded. This was an expensive boutique hotel located about thirty minutes from here. "He has to stay somewhere and—"

"Millie Topper is staying there too. In the same room."

"How do you know that?"

"They were having a drink in the cocktail lounge next to the lobby. I went inside and positioned myself at a table nearby."

"But they must have recognized you." I said, raising my voice slightly.

My mother shook her head. "Not at all. Remember, at the dinner and sales meeting, Millie never left the dais the entire night. She never met or saw me."

"But Austin—"

"I wore a disguise," my mother said.

I almost spilled my coffee. Archie stirred but only a bit. "What type of disguise?"

"The last few days, when I was with Marcia, I began to get suspicious. I started believing what you and Matt said about it being a scam." My mother sat back in her chair. "I decided I would investigate the night of the dinner and sales meeting."

"So, this was planned?"

She nodded. "I bought a wig and put it on in the car after the dinner. You'd be surprised how a different hair color and style can totally change your appearance. Casual acquaintances usually don't recognize you. And Austin is only a casual acquaintance."

My mother sipped her coffee. "To make sure I wouldn't be recognized, I also put on my reading glasses and took off the blue cardigan I'd been wearing at the dinner meeting. It was so cold at the cocktail lounge, but I didn't want him to recognize the sweater."

I smiled. My mother, now adjusted to Florida weather, liked

it hot. She constantly fiddled with my air conditioning, always raising the thermostat.

"You're sure they didn't recognize you?" I asked.

"Positive. It turns out I didn't have to go to that much trouble with a disguise either. We couldn't see each other. A huge potted plant separated our tables. But I could hear everything they said."

I rose and shook my foot, numb from Archie cutting off circulation.

"Back to my original question," I said as I maneuvered around the table to refill my coffee mug. "How do you know they were staying in the same room? Maybe they just met in the lounge to discuss business while having a drink."

My mother sighed and shook her head as if I should know better. I remember her doing this when I was a child.

"When they finished their drinks, Millie said she left her key card in her room and asked Austin if he had his. He said he did. I also checked at the front desk. I said I wanted to leave a note for Mille Topper. The desk clerk said there was no one by that name, so I described her and the man she was with."

"Did the clerk know whom you meant?"

"Oh, yes. He said I must mean Millie Wells."

"Austin and Mille Wells? Husband and wife? Brother and sister?"

"By the way he kissed her, I'm pretty sure it's husband and wife."

"Did you find out anything else? I'm trying to locate the factory that manufactures their products."

My mother grinned again. "I may have the answer. While sipping their cocktails, Austin mentioned to Millie that he was going back home in the morning. He said he'd be back the following day."

"Home could be where the factory is located," I said.

"My thoughts exactly."

"Did he say where he was headed?"

My mother nodded. "Tarrytown, New York."

Bingo!

CHAPTER 24

On Monday afternoon I stepped into the *Animal Advocate Magazine* office and was confronted by a blast of frigid air. The air-conditioning system had been set on high. That meant our editor wasn't here. Olivia hated cold.

"What's wrong," I asked Clara, who sat behind her desk staring into space with furrowed brows.

"Olivia phoned. She got called into a meeting in Manhattan with corporate."

My stomach churned. Meeting with the bigwigs who owned *Animal Advocate* was never good. It usually meant budget cuts or changes in how we operated.

"She didn't sound like she was in a great mood," Clara added as she scratched her head, oblivious to the mess it made of her short gray hair.

"Olivia never sounds like she is in a great mood," I said. Our editor was one gruff, no-nonsense lady who'd worked her way up from the streets of the south Bronx. But she always had our backs. I wouldn't want another editor.

"We can only adopt a 'wait and see' attitude." I shrugged and made my way to my cubicle.

I spent the first hour writing up part of my story on the sanctuary. But I couldn't concentrate. I kept conjuring up images of Maureen McDermott's body in the bear enclosure.

I remembered back to the conversation I overheard before the body had been discovered. Sam asked Nick to fire Maureen and hire him full time. If Sam had murdered Maureen, there would be no reason to ask that.

But could it have been an act on Sam's part to throw suspicion off him?

Next, I thought back on Nick's reply to Sam, "She may be gone sooner than you realize." What did that mean?

Finally, I thought about alibis. Detective Fox told me alibis would be almost impossible to verify. The key word was "almost." I needed to find out from Fox where each suspect claimed to be at the time of the murder. Maybe I could find a hole in someone's alibi.

I sat back in my chair and began to ponder motives. Maureen's accusation threatened Declan's career. With her gone, that charge went away.

Nick Lamonica was unable to visit his children because of the lucrative divorce settlement Maureen obtained for his wife. Revenge was a strong motive.

But Nick wasn't the only one who might seek revenge. Maureen destroyed Sam Garcia's father's restaurant. Sam said his father wound up selling the business.

How much of a financial loss was incurred?

How deeply did Sam feel about the loss of his family's restaurant?

What about Lee and Gina? Aside from not liking Maureen, was there a deeper motive for wanting her dead?

I needed to dig deeper into their lives.

Next, I began thinking about Declan and the missing etorphine.

Who could have taken it?

How?

I punched in Declan's number on my phone and was able to

reach him.

"The other day you said the veterinary infirmary is locked when you're out, right?"

"Absolutely."

"But staff is permitted inside when you're there."

"Yes. The keepers want to check on their animals that are in for treatment."

"What about Gina and Lee?"

"They don't drop in as much as the keepers, but they do stop by. Gina sometimes photographs an animal for the newsletter, and Lee conducts random inventory."

"When staff is there, are you constantly with them?"

He hesitated. "Most of the time."

I sucked in my breath. "But not always?"

"If I'm in the operating area, I might not notice if someone entered."

"A while back you told me the medicine is locked up, right?"

"Yes."

"Where's the key?"

"Usually with me, but..." He paused.

"What?"

"Before I start any operation or treatment, I take the medicine I need and bring it with me. But while I'm operating, I leave the medicine cabinet open in case I need to get more."

"Would you have noticed if someone was near the cabinet?"

"The cabinet is in the front. The operating table is in the back room."

I had nothing more to ask now. After saying good-bye, I pondered my conversation with Declan. Could someone have snuck in while Declan was in the operating area? My thoughts were interrupted when Clara burst into my cubicle.

"Olivia phoned again," she said. "She's calling an all staff meeting for ten o'clock sharp on Wednesday. You'll get an email. All staff must attend."

It felt like tiny spiders crawling in my stomach. While Olivia held a staff meeting on the first day of every month, an impromptu staff meeting was different. This meant something big was happening.

And that was never good.

CHAPTER 25

M y phone trilled. Abby's name popped up on my screen.
"Are you free after work?" she asked. "If so, why don't
we do some bridal gown shopping? I'd love to go to Flower
Grove Bridal Salon. I heard their dresses are gorgeous."

I smiled. My mother was having dinner with a few of her
friends from her old neighborhood. Abby knew this would be
one of the rare occasions we could get together without her—or
at least without hurting her feelings.

"Great idea," I said. "Text the address, and I'll meet you there
in an hour."

A few seconds later, I received her text. The bridal shop was
located on Randall Street in the Village of Scallop Bay Cove. For
some reason, that address rang a bell, but I didn't know why.

Abby and I met by the bridal shop at the appointed time.
Randall Street was lined with old trees, Victorian styled
streetlamps, wrought iron benches and hanging flower pots.
The air smelled of salt water. No surprise since the Atlantic
Ocean was only a few minutes away.

"This place is going to be expensive," I mumbled. Abby
apparently didn't hear me.

We made our way into the store. My daughter tried on several
gowns, but she found something about each one she didn't like.

"Please don't let her become a Bridezilla," I mumbled. This

time I think she heard me. She grinned.

"I have at least seven more shops I want to check out," Abby said when we exited the store two hours later.

I groaned.

"But not tonight. Let's get something to eat. There's a restaurant right there," Abby said, pointing to a place called *Ships Galley.*

Suddenly, it dawned on me why Randall Street in Scallop Bay Cove sounded familiar. It was the former location of El Mar, the restaurant owned by Sam Garcia's father.

Sam said it had opened under new ownership. "Yes. Let's definitely go there."

"Mom, what are you up to?" My daughter probably could tell by the enthusiasm in my voice that this had to do with more than food.

I told her about El Mar and Sam Garcia's father. "When a new restaurant opens where a previous one closed, the new owner will often keep former employees."

"And you're hoping some of the wait staff may have worked for Sam's father." Abby finished my thought. "You want to talk to them. Isn't that a long shot?"

I shrugged. "Maybe. But we need to eat anyway. C'mon."

The restaurant had a nautical theme with light blue walls and white trim. It was decorated with anchors, nets, and seascapes. Since it was Monday night, not a popular night for eating out on Long Island, the place was only half full.

"I often came here when this place was El Mar," I lied to the hostess who picked up menus and was about to seat us. "I'm wondering if any of the old wait staff is still here. They were wonderful."

"Most are new, but James is a holdover," she said.

"I think I remember him," I lied again. "I'd love to sit in the area he serves—for old time's sake."

"I have some former El Mar customers," the hostess said as we passed a server with the name tag *James.*

He stared at us as if he had no idea who we were, which was true.

Once seated, he took our drink orders. He had a stork-like build and thinning brown hair that he combed over to give the impression he wasn't going bald. It didn't work.

"You were here under the old owners, right?" I asked before he had a chance to leave. "When this place was El Mar?"

He nodded. "Yes. The new owner kept some of us on. It's hard to get experienced help."

James appeared to scan the room. "Most of the others have moved on. I'm the only one aside from two of the kitchen workers who's still on staff."

"Do you like working here?"

"It's good." He shrugged. "The new owner treats everyone okay. But the old owner treated us like family. It's a shame what happened."

"I heard about the roaches," I said, sympathetically.

"They were planted. That woman destroyed him. I better put in your order."

As he moved away, Abby asked, "What do you hope to find out?"

"I'm not sure. But I've already learned something. He said, 'that woman destroyed him.' I'm sure he was referring to Maureen. If the staff knew she planted the roaches, Oscar Garcia had to know. This confirms what I thought."

James returned with our drinks—the usual, my pomegranate martini and the house white wine for Abby.

"Do you still keep in contact with the Garcia family?" I asked.

"I did at first, but not much anymore." He shook his head. "Oscar had a heart attack the night after the health department closed him down. He recovered, but his heart was damaged.

The next year, he had another heart attack. This one killed him. I think the financial strain was too much."

"I knew he went out of business, but I didn't know the extent of his financial situation," I said.

"Up until the roach incident, the restaurant was doing so well Oscar decided to redo the kitchen and upgrade the dining room. He took out a huge loan and put his house up as collateral."

I sucked in my breath. "Did he lose his home?"

James nodded. "And he also lost the money he had put away for his retirement. I think the stress was too much. At least that's what his son Sam says. He blames the loss of the restaurant for his father's death."

CHAPTER 26

The next morning, when I stepped inside the administration building at the Happy Place Animal Sanctuary, the chair behind the receptionist's desk was occupied by a young woman. She was slight of build and looked like a high school student, but I had a feeling she was older.

"I'm Wendy Wu, administrative assistant to the director," she said, after I introduced myself. A broad smile appeared on her face. "I was on vacation last week, but I heard all about you from Gina when I came back here yesterday."

"You missed quite a week," I said.

"I know. But I had a fabulous time at the Jersey shore." Her grin widened but then quickly faded. "I heard what happened to Maureen. It's horrible."

I nodded and asked, "What do you do here?"

"I handle scheduling and data entry. I also assist with the newsletter and anything else Gina gives me to do. Sometimes, I pitch in and help with the animals, which I love. I hope to become a veterinarian, and any experience with animals looks great on my resume."

She talked at warp speed. I didn't know if I could get a word in, but I tried. "My daughter and husband are veterinarians," I said. "If you want to talk to one of them, I can—"

"I'd love that. Declan Carr, our veterinarian, has taken me

under his wing too. Sometimes, when I finish in the office, I'll head to the veterinary infirmary and help him out."

She paused, apparently to catch her breath. "I'm a part-time employee. I'm only at the receptionist desk from 8:00 AM till 1:00 PM. My classes at Harper University don't start until 5:00 PM, so unless I need to study for a test. I have oodles of time to spend volunteering and learning from Declan."

Classes at the university. I knew she was older than she looked.

"If you work with the animals, you must know the keepers too."

She nodded.

"Did you deal much with Maureen McDermott?"

"Absolutely. If I'm not volunteering with Declan, I would usually wind up working with Maureen and the animals that weren't dangerous. Of course, all animals can be dangerous, but you know what I mean." Wendy's eyes twinkled. "I would be sent nowhere near wolves or crocodiles."

"I understand Maureen was difficult."

Wendy hesitated. "I really shouldn't say anything."

"I'm not going to print this, but I need to get a better picture of Maureen."

Wendy furrowed her brows but then answered. "She was demanding, and she possessed a sharp tongue. But I could handle her. When Maureen was particularly grouchy, I'd talk about the antics of my two cats. That always put her in a better mood."

"I heard that friction between Maureen and Gina escalated recently. What do you think caused that?"

"I don't think I should say anything. It's gossip. And you are a reporter even if you go off the record."

I decided the best approach was to be honest. I needed to find out who murdered Maureen, and I didn't believe it was Declan.

Since Wendy appeared fond of Declan, maybe she would help.

"The police are looking at Declan as a person of interest," I said.

She gasped. "No way. Declan would never murder anyone."

"I agree. But the only way to help him is by finding the real murderer. And gossip often hides a smidgen of truth."

Wendy remained silent for a moment but finally spoke up. "In the beginning, Maureen and Gina appeared okay with each other. But that suddenly changed. For the last two months, Gina became critical of everything Maureen did or said."

"That was around the time of Gina's dad's death, right?"

Wendy nodded. "When Gina returned from work after the funeral, she did a total turnaround with Maureen."

"Did something happen at the funeral?"

Wendy shrugged. "All the sanctuary staff went to the memorial service for Gina's dad. When we arrived at the church, Gina greeted Maureen and the rest of us cordially. It was at the end of the service when I saw a reaction."

"What happened at the end?"

"Gina, her mother, and other family members formed a receiving line by the church's front doors. The look in her eyes when Maureen approached…" Wendy shook her head. "I've never seen eyes display such anger."

"Why would Gina react that way?"

"Oh, it wasn't Gina. The death stare came from Gina's mom."

CHAPTER 27

The connection was Gina's mom. Dozens of scenarios flashed through my mind, but they were only theories. I had to find out more about Gina's parents.

My thoughts were interrupted by a loud, "Good Morning."

Gina Garone strutted into the building. Wendy shot me a look that I interpreted as "don't let Gina know she was the topic of our conversation." I winked at Wendy to assure her that I never divulge a source.

"I see you've met," Gina said as she approached the receptionist desk. "I've wonderful news. Ticket sales for our next fundraiser have surpassed our expectations."

Gina turned toward me. "Why don't you come into my office, and I'll tell you more."

I followed Gina as she breezed into her office. Once seated, she updated me on the garden party scheduled for this Friday.

"It will be fabulous. The food is coming from the top caterer on Long Island, and we'll have loads of raffles. Why don't you come as my guest?"

"I'd love to attend." I suddenly had an idea. "May I let you know definitely this afternoon? I want to make sure my mother doesn't have plans for me. She's up from Florida visiting me." I hoped this would be a good segue into families, and that I could steer the conversation toward Gina's parents.

"Absolutely. Call me later."

"I enjoy my mom's visits," I went on to say. "It's hard when family is far away. Is your family near you?"

"Just my husband now. My son is away at boarding school, and my mom lives in New Jersey." She paused. "My dad died earlier this year."

"I'm sorry. Were you born in New Jersey, or did your parents move there later?"

"I was born on Long Island. We lived in Sands Point, but we moved to New Jersey when I was around twelve years old. I came back here for college, which is where I met my husband, We've been here ever since."

"I've relatives in Jersey," I said. "Whereabouts did you live?"

She hesitated before speaking. "Wayside."

Her first home in Sands Point was one of the most exclusive communities on Long Island. People who lived there had money—lots of money. I knew about Wayside New Jersey, too. I'd passed it several times on the way to visit an aunt who lived further south. Wayside was a blue collar working class community.

Something must have happened to Gina's family's finances to cause such a move.

I vaguely remembered from my initial research of Gina that her maiden name was Molinaro. I'd do more research on her parents later today.

After leaving the sanctuary, I headed to the *Animal Advocate* office. Clara was not at her desk, so I grabbed a cup of coffee and bee-lined to my cubicle before she returned and bombarded me with questions.

I booted up my computer. It didn't take long until I found the obituary for Gina's dad.

The elder Molinaro, whose first name was Gregory, had been a used car salesman in Wayside, New Jersey. It was his previous profession from when he lived in Sands Point that shocked me.

He had been a lawyer.

He had been disbarred.

CHAPTER 28

As an attorney, did he have contact with Maureen? Had they been professional adversaries? Did she play a role in his disbarment?

I grabbed my phone and punched in a number.

Matt's patients included an Old English bulldog owned by Stan Margolis, one of the top lawyers on Long Island. He was prominent in the bar association—the lawyer, not the bulldog. If anyone could find out about the disbarment of Gina's father, he could.

Luckily, he was able to answer my call. I told him what I was looking for, and he said he'd get back to me.

I'd no sooner disconnected from Stan when my phone trilled. My mother's name popped up.

This can't be good.

My mother zoomed right to the point. "Good news. I've arranged a meeting for you with Fran Foote."

"Who is Fran Foote?"

"Fran is another Ajax Pet Products investor. Before you arrived at Sunday's dinner and sales meeting, Fran and I chatted. Let's say, she's not a satisfied customer."

"Okay. When is the meeting?"

"In an hour. It's part of your work, right? You're writing a story on the scam."

"Absolutely. I'll be there." I received an email yesterday from my editor approving this topic.

My mother gave me Fran's address. I finished a few odds and ends at my desk, shut down my computer, and departed my cubicle. I'd get back to researching Gina Garone's father later.

On the way out, I ran into Clara who had returned to her desk.

"Don't forget tomorrow's staff meeting with Olivia. Ten o'clock sharp," she called out.

"Has Olivia said what it's about?"

"No." Clara looked over her half-moon glasses. "And that's a bad sign."

Fran Foote lived in a retirement community in eastern Long Island. When I arrived my mother was there.

"Is Marcia coming?" I asked as Fran headed into the kitchen to get us coffee.

My mother shook her head. "No. I didn't tell her about this. She still believes Ajax is a legitimate company. I thought I'd wait until we have more evidence."

"OK." I no sooner sat on the sofa when a large gray cat hopped on my lap.

"That's Gretel," Fran said as she stepped into the living room carrying a tray containing three steaming mugs of coffee. "Hansel is hiding under my bed. He rarely comes out when company is here."

Fran was a large woman with a ruddy complexion and short gray hair that matched the cat. While Gretel fanned me with her tail, I asked Fran how she got involved with Ajax Pet Products.

"I saw an ad posted for a dinner and a chance to get rich."

"Have you sold any franchises?"

Fran shook her head. "None. Ajax plastered their

advertisements for the dinner and sales meeting throughout the town, especially in this housing complex. It appears that anyone who was interested attended the meeting and invested. There no one left to sell to except for family." She sighed. "I have no family left."

"What about products? Did you sell any items from the catalog?"

"I sold seven items for a total of two hundred dollars." She grimaced. "I made twenty dollars commission. But I've stopped selling. It was a horrible experience."

"What do you mean?"

"A few items were never delivered, and I had the worst time getting money back for my customers. I contacted the Ajax sales manager, but he said he couldn't help. He said all companies had glitches. I think this was more than a glitch."

She scowled and continued. "To make matters worse, he berated me for pushing the merchandise. He said I should stick to selling franchises."

"What did you do?"

I ended up refunding my neighbor out of my own pocket. And the products that did arrive weren't worth the money."

"How so?"

"One of the ladies I play cards with purchased a brush for her Yorkshire terrier. Her adult daughter has a similar brush for her Pomeranian—she's says the brushes are identical—only she bought hers from Omega Animal Grooming Supplies and paid half of what the Ajax brush cost."

"I wonder," I mumbled as I jotted a reminder to locate and visit the Ajax factory upstate.

"Wonder what?" my mother asked.

"Oh, nothing." But a scenario squirreled through my mind.

I realized I might be uncovering a bigger fraud than the pyramid scheme.

CHAPTER 29

I was the first to arrive at the *Animal Advocate* office the next morning. I settled down in my cubicle with a mug of steaming coffee, grabbed my cell phone, and punched in the number for Detective Fox.

"Something is bothering me," I said, after we exchanged greetings. "How could the killer take a chance that the murder wouldn't be seen by another sanctuary employee?"

"Because the staff follows a set daily routine—a routine which is widely known. Five sanctuary employees, in addition to the victim, were on the grounds at the time of the murder, and not one of them was scheduled to be near the bear exhibit until after eight."

"So, the murderer could be pretty sure that no one else would be there."

"Right. First, the keepers pick up the daily animal food from the storage building, which is located at the northern most end of the sanctuary. Then they work their way down. No one hits the area near the bear until at least an hour later."

"What about Declan?"

"Same thing. Declan goes straight to the veterinary infirmary and usually stays there for an hour."

"But this time, he was with the deer, right?"

"That's what he claims. The deer habitat is on the way to the

109

infirmary. That's how he spotted one in distress."

"And I assume the deer and the infirmary are not near the bear." I paused. "But what about Lee or Gina? Couldn't they be anywhere on the grounds?"

"Not really," Fox said. "According to Lee, he spends most of his time in his office. If he leaves, it's only to go to the veterinary infirmary, the supply building, or the food storage center. All of those locations are nowhere near the bear enclosure. The morning of the murder, Lee claims he went to the infirmary, and Declan wasn't there."

"Why did he go to the infirmary?"

"I don't know." I could hear Fox sigh. "Wolfe interviewed him but didn't put the reason in his notes."

I jotted down a reminder to ask Lee about this.

"What about Gina?" I asked.

"She claims she rarely leaves the office, except for public relations photo shoots and escorting prospective donors around the grounds."

"She left that morning," I said. "I was with her a few minutes after seven o'clock when she answered a phone call and rushed out."

"I know all about it. On the morning of the murder, she was contacted by her neighbor. Gina's dog had escaped from the house and was outside. She thinks her husband probably left the door open when he went to get the newspaper and didn't realize the dog had gotten out. Gina lives about five minutes away. She left the sanctuary immediately, picked up her dog, who had only gone a short distance down the road, and brought him home. She returned to the sanctuary around seven-thirty."

"Why didn't she just ask her neighbor to take in the dog?"

"Her neighbor walks with a cane and could never catch him."

I sipped my coffee and thought for a moment. "You said she returned at seven-thirty. How does she account for her time after that?"

"She claims she went back to her office and stayed there for about thirty minutes. After that, she left the building. She had decided to feature Bella in this month's newsletter, so she needed to take a photo of the bear."

Fox hesitated and then continued. "It is a bit unusual. I was told she normally notifies one of the keepers when she intends to photograph an animal. But she said this was a spur of the moment decision. She headed out to the bear habitat around eight o'clock, knowing Nick would be getting to Bella around that time."

"I heard her scream around eight-ten. I'm guessing that's when she arrived at the bear habitat and saw the dead body. The medical examiner puts the time of death within an hour before the body was discovered, right?" I asked.

"Yes. I'm guessing Maureen was killed before eight to be sure no one would be there."

I frowned. "Except no one could be sure Gina wouldn't show up. It seems her schedule is more flexible than the others. She could decide on a whim to take a picture."

"It would be a risk, but a low risk. As I mentioned before, Gina rarely leaves the office."

"But she did on the day of the murder." A question popped into my mind. "On the morning Maureen was killed, Gina returned to the sanctuary at seven-thirty. Would that give her enough time to commit murder?"

"Seven-thirty to eight is tight, but yes, it's possible," he replied. He sighed. "No alibis can be proven, but none can be refuted either."

"So far," I added and said good-bye.

I sat back, sipped my coffee, and was deep in thought when my phone trilled again. This call was from my attorney contact, Stan Margolis.

"Did you find out anything on Gina Garone's father?" I asked after we exchanged pleasantries, and I inquired about the well-being of Rocky, his bulldog.

"Rocky's fine. He's sleeping under my desk and snoring." Stan chuckled and then got to the point of his call. "Molinari was disbarred for lying on his law school application and on his form for admittance to the New York bar. When asked if he had ever been convicted of a crime, he answered no. But he had a shoplifting conviction from his freshman year of college. He applied to a prestigious law school and figured if he told the truth he wouldn't get in."

"He was disbarred for shoplifting?"

"No. For lying about it." Stan paused. "He was a well-respected lawyer for more than fifteen years before his lie was exposed."

"How was it exposed?"

"By another lawyer who reported it to the bar association. Molinari was handling a divorce for a friend. The lawyer for his client's spouse did what is known as opposition research, not only on her client's ex-husband but on his attorney."

I'd heard of opposition research. The purpose was to dig up as much dirt as possible. It was used a lot in politics, but lately it appeared to be used whenever someone wanted to smear another person's reputation.

I was pretty sure I knew the identity of the other attorney, but I asked anyway.

"Maureen McDermott," Stan answered.

After saying good-bye, another thought popped into my mind. Did Maureen use a private investigator to dig up dirt? Maureen's administrative assistant, Joyce, should know this. I grabbed my phone and punched in her number.

"Yes. Maureen had a private investigator on retainer," Joyce said after I explained the reason for my call. "His name is Jake Spano."

"Do you know how I can reach him?" I thought he might be a good source of information.

"I have his contact information. I'll text it to you."

I decided to refill my mug before I called Jake. As I made my way toward the coffee maker, I passed Clara who was slouched in her chair behind her desk. There were tears in her eyes.

"What's wrong?"

She sniffed. "Olivia's been in a car accident. She's in the hospital. Our editor is in a coma."

CHAPTER 30

Before I left the house the next morning, I phoned Clara for an update on Olivia. Nothing new. She was still in a coma.

"Is there anything I can do?" I asked.

"Pray for her."

And I did.

I finished my third coffee, filled my travel mug with more of the caffeine-laden drink, and drove off. After a few errands, I headed to the sanctuary and arrived mid-day. The skies were overcast, so in case of a summer storm, I brought my umbrella.

Wendy Wu was sitting behind the reception desk. She appeared to be staring into space, and she was frowning.

"Good morning," I called.

She spun her head in my direction. "Oh, hello. I didn't see you enter."

"Everything okay?" I asked.

"Of course. I'm fine. Can I help you?"

When I first met Wendy, I would have described her personality as bubbly. But not today.

"I wanted to talk to Gina," I said. I planned to question all five suspects and hopefully find a hole in one of the alibis. I thought I'd start my quest at the top with the director.

"She's not here. She's at a meeting with a prospective donor." Wendy fiddled with her necklace. It was the letter "W" on a gold chain. I remembered it from the first day we met.

"Then I'll catch up with Gina another time. What about Lee? Is he here?"

"Yes. Let me see if he's available." She picked up her desk phone and dialed what I assumed was Lee's extension.

Whatever he said made her wince. A few seconds later, she pressed the hold button. "He's pretty busy. Do you want to make the appointment for another day?"

"I only need a few minutes of his time, and I'm on a deadline."

"I'll see what I can do." Wendy asked him again. This time he agreed to see me as long as I kept it short.

"I thought we finished our interview," he said as I stepped through his doorway. He was typing on his computer keyboard and didn't look away when he spoke.

"Just a few more questions." I slid into a chair across from him. "I heard you went to the veterinary infirmary on the morning when Maureen was killed. I'm curious why a business manager would visit the infirmary."

"I wanted to question Declan about some supplies he ordered." Lee continued typing.

"Why not talk to him by phone?"

"I prefer to drop in unannounced. While I'm there, I perform a spot check inventory on his medicines."

Lee finally stopped typing and looked away from his computer screen. Facing me now, he continued talking. "Declan keeps a log. Each time he uses a drug, he lists the dosage in the book. I frequently monitor his current inventory and his log. I want to make sure all medicines have been accounted for, especially controlled substances. A lot of these drugs can fetch a pretty penny on the black market."

I recalled Declan telling me that Lee stopped by on a random basis for inventory. To me, this provided another reason why Declan wouldn't steal the etorphine. Declan knew Lee could pop in at any moment. If Declan was stealing drugs, Lee would find out sooner or later and report him. It didn't make sense.

"Have you ever found a discrepancy?" I asked.

He hesitated before answering. "No."

A thought that had been back somewhere in my subconscious suddenly sprang forward. I was annoyed and sure my face showed it. "Did you feel doing inventory that morning was more important than keeping your appointment with me? Gina told me something came up unexpectedly. I thought it was an emergency and—"

"I totally forgot our appointment." He held up his hands. "I had almost reached the infirmary when I remembered it. But if I rushed back to the office, I might not be able to do the inventory at all that day. So I texted Gina to ask you to postpone until later. I apologize."

Lee sat back in his swivel chair. "Declan must be present when I conduct the drug check. He's always there at seven, but after eight, he could be anywhere in the sanctuary. And since the inventory is a done as a surprise, I can't make an appointment."

"But Declan wasn't there, was he? What did you do?"

"I waited outside for about ten minutes. Then I took a stroll through the grounds. As business manager it's important to know the condition of the facilities. After that, I arrived back at the office to wait for you. I was there when I heard the ambulance and police sirens."

"Was Gina in the office when you returned?"

He shook his head. "No. I arrived back about eight-fifteen. She had left. The bear habitat is located to the south, and I was coming from the north, so we never crossed paths."

"Was it unusual that Declan was not at the infirmary when you went there that morning?"

"First time it happened. His routine was to head to the veterinary infirmary as soon as he arrived at the sanctuary.

He'd stay there for at least an hour."

"Did you call or text him to find out where he was?"

"I did call, but it went straight to voice mail. If the name of someone involved with the animals had popped up, Declan would have answered in a nanosecond. But with my name showing on the screen, he let it go to voice mail." Lee narrowed his eyes in what I interpreted as a show of annoyance. "Declan doesn't consider anything I do urgent."

Lee glanced at his watch. "Do you have any more questions?"

"Did you get the inventory done?"

"Not that day. With the murder of a staff member, we all were preoccupied with other matters including the police investigation."

I found it interesting that he referred to Maureen as "staff member," and not by her name.

I figured I'd gotten all I could from him today. We said our good-byes and I made my way out of his office to the reception area. Wendy appeared to be staring at a notebook on her desk.

"I'll stop by at some other time to see Gina," I told her.

"Okay." That was all she said, and she didn't look up at me when she said it.

I emerged from the building and was pondering my next course of action when Declan appeared on my horizon. I called to him. "Do you have a minute to talk?"

"I'm on my way back to the infirmary," he said. "Why don't you walk with me?"

I joined him. Since Declan was more than six feet tall, and I was only five feet, I had to hurry to keep up with his long strides.

"It's a long trek," Declan said. "I could drive there, but I enjoy the exercise."

The overcast day had turned to sunny with blue skies. We walked a way until I realized I'd left my umbrella in Lee's office. I didn't want to ask Declan to wait while I retrieved it, so I decided I'd pick it up on my way out.

"Are you related to a Regina Carr?" I asked as we trekked up the path.

"She's my aunt. Why do you ask?"

"Apparently, Maureen McDermott knew her. Were you aware of that?"

Declan shook his head. "Aunt Regina and I are not particularly close anymore. With her schedule and my schedule, we've been too busy. I haven't seen her probably in three years."

He may not have kept in touch, but I bet Maureen knew of the relationship.

"Do you know how to contact your aunt?" I asked.

He nodded. "I have her address, email, and phone number."

"Could you give it to me? I'd like to speak with her."

"Why?"

I told Declan that I had spoken to Maureen's former administrative assistant who told me Maureen knew Regina. If there was friction between the two women, Maureen might have taken it out on Declan. I wanted to find out.

"I don't see how this will help with the murder case." He scratched his head.

I wasn't sure either. But I was firmly convinced that the more I knew about Maureen McDermott, the closer I'd get to finding out why she was killed.

Declan gave me his aunt's contact information. She lived in Scarsdale, a northern suburb of New York.

We reached the infirmary and were greeted by a load roar.

"That's our mountain lion," Declan said, grinning. "Her injured paw is almost completely healed, and she's impatient to get out of the cage and go back in her habitat."

I surveyed my surroundings. The main room consisted of a large desk and three cabinets with signage reading: *medicines, supplies, food.*

There were also several cages. Only two were occupied. One held a monkey and the other a wallaby.

"The operating area is in the back, and it's adjacent to a room that holds larger cages. That's where the mountain lion is recuperating," Declan said.

"What if you need to keep a huge animal, like the bear or giraffe?"

We have holding cages outside that—"

Declan's phone rang. He answered. As he listened to his caller, his face froze. "I'll be right there."

"Two wolves escaped. The two sisters," he said. "They're by the llama enclosure trying to find a way to enter." Declan grabbed his tranquillizer gun. "You need to stay here."

He headed to the door, but halfway there he stopped and turned toward me. "I know I said no one is allowed in the infirmary when I'm not here, but this is an emergency. Don't leave until I text you it's safe."

"How did the wolves get out?"

"I don't know. I have to go. Remember, don't leave the building," he said again as he slammed the door shut with me inside.

I paced around the room. Then I made a decision. I scooted out the door.

"I probably shouldn't do this," I mumbled, but my journalistic instinct told me I had to find out how the wolves escaped.

I made sure the lock was on when I shut the infirmary door behind me. The last thing Declan needed was someone sneaking in and stealing more drugs.

I grabbed the sanctuary map from my tote bag. As I hurried down the path I reasoned with myself. The wolves were outside the llama enclosure. Since Declan knew this, he should have them tranquilized by now.

How could it be dangerous?

Nevertheless, I felt my heart pounding as I made my way, constantly alert for signs of wolves.

I heard a rustling sound in the bushes.

I froze.

A squirrel emerged.

I continued hurrying down the path, always checking my surroundings. The sanctuary housed three llamas and I remembered what I'd learned about them. Two, including Manfred the spitter, were young with powerful hooves. But the third llama was old and arthritic. He had been rescued from a petting zoo that was planning on euthanizing him because his upkeep was expensive. This llama wouldn't stand a chance against the two wolves. I hoped Declan made it in time.

I finally approached the llama enclosure. Nick, assisted by Declan and Sam, were loading a wolf into what appeared to be a portable cage in the back of a pick-up truck. Although I'd seen these animals at a distance, I hadn't realized until now how huge and powerful they were.

I wiped the perspiration off my forehead and breathed a sigh of relief at the sight of Declan securing the wolf in the cage.

Then, with horror, I realized the second cage was empty. Only one wolf had been captured.

CHAPTER 31

Declan spotted me. He marched in my direction, a frown spread across his face and his lips pursed in anger.

"I told you to stay put."

"Where's the other wolf?" I asked, ignoring his comment.

"We don't know. When I arrived only the one wolf was here, which is highly unusual. Wolves travel together."

A howl came from the other side. From what I'd read, I guessed this was probably the missing wolf communicating her location to her sister.

"Let's head in the direction of the wolf call," Nick yelled.

"You can't stay here alone," Declan said to me. "Get in the truck."

Declan and I hopped in the truck and followed Nick. We made our way around the bend, and there she stood.

The wolf perched high on a rock.

"Stay in the truck," Declan ordered. He hopped out.

The wolf's fur stood on end as she bared her teeth and emitted a low growl.

I recalled an article explaining how incidents of wolves attacking humans were low. Most were caused by rabid wolves, and the wolves at the animal sanctuary were certainly not rabid.

But wolf attacks did occur, and this wolf looked ready to spring into action.

I shivered.

Suddenly, something shot through the air. The wolf fell to the ground. Declan had tranquilized the powerful animal.

As Nick and Declan loaded the wolf into the cage, a familiar voice called out, "Nick, what happened?"

I glanced to my left and saw Gina Garone. Nick hurried in her direction.

Since the wolf was secured, I made my way toward Declan. "C'mon," I whispered. "Let's go over there and listen."

We were fairly close to Nick and Gina, but we moved nearer to ensure we could hear all that was said.

"The wolves broke a portion of their fence," Nick told Gina.

"You're responsible for insuring all our fences are secure." Gina scowled. "That's a top priority."

"I inspected it yesterday, and it was fine."

"Then how did this happen?"

Nick shrugged. "I've no idea."

I exchanged glances with Declan. "Either Nick has been derelict in his duties, or someone sabotaged the fence," I whispered.

"Sabotage? Why?"

"I don't know but it may be related to Maureen's murder."

Declan shook his head. "Then again, it may not."

I wasn't sure, so I didn't want to argue.

"I'll replace the fence now," Nick said to Gina. "We'll be able to transport the two wolves back to their enclosure before the tranquilizer wears off."

"See that you do," Gina ordered. "And before you leave today, check all of the enclosures to make sure they are secure."

Nick nodded. "I will. But we still need to hire—"

"I'm working on getting another part-time keeper," she said. "In the meantime, we have volunteers who can work with the smaller animals while you and Sam Garcia can handle the larger ones."

"Don't forget, George broke his foot hiking in the Adirondacks. He won't be back for quite some time," Nick reminded her.

I remembered hearing there was an animal keeper who had been on vacation since before the murder. I assumed this was George. Nick appeared to have his hands full. I wondered if the lack of staff was creating a dangerous situation.

As Gina turned to leave, she spotted me. She did not look pleased.

"More research?" she asked, her voice dripping with sarcasm.

"Yes. I wanted to speak to you, but I can see you have other things on your mind. We'll do it another day." I smiled. "I thought you were at a meeting."

"I was leaving the meeting when I got the text from Nick. Staff is required to contact me immediately if and when an incident occurs. Now, please excuse me. I have urgent matters at hand."

I figured there was no reason for me to stay. It looked like everyone would be busy for the rest of the day. I was heading back to my car when I remembered my umbrella was still in Lee's office, so I made my way back there.

When I entered the administration building, Wendy was still ensconced behind her desk. Her head faced downward, and she appeared to be writing. I don't think she noticed yet that I was there. I can be quiet as a mouse.

"Glad someone your age knows how to use a pen," I joked as I approached her desk and saw that she was scribbling something in a notebook. "I thought your generation wrote everything on the computer."

Wendy looked up and flinched. She quickly closed the notebook.

"I forgot my umbrella, and I want to grab it from Lee's office,"

I said.

"Of course. I'll get it for you." She rose from her chair.

But before she left, she stashed the notebook in her top drawer.

CHAPTER 32

The smell of burning bread permeated the room. Matt wandered into the kitchen where I was leaning over the sink scrapping off the black top of an English muffin. It had been in the toaster too long.

Matt grinned.

I looked down at the muffin and then broke it in two. I gave the pieces to Archie and Brandy who were at my side. They never criticized my culinary abilities.

"How about I make eggs?" Matt said.

I shook my head. "Thanks. But I better get to work. I'll grab some cereal."

After a demolishing a bowl of Cheerios, I phoned Clara, but it went straight to voice mail. I left a message asking if there was any change in Olivia's condition.

After that I phoned Regina Carr. I explained that I was a reporter doing a story on the Happy Place Animal Sanctuary.

"My nephew is a veterinarian there." She chuckled. "But I'm sure you know that."

Declan and his Aunt Regina may not have kept close contact, but she appeared aware of what he was doing.

"I heard you were acquainted with one of the animal keepers. Maureen McDermott," I said, getting back to the reason for my call. "I was hoping we could get together, and I could speak to you about her."

"Do you want to know if I think Declan murdered her?"

I was taken aback and momentarily silent.

'It's all over the news, and I've been following the story," she went on to say. "From what I've read, Declan was one of five employees at the sanctuary when the murder occurred. Of course, he's a suspect. But I don't believe for a moment he did it."

"I agree." We chatted about Declan, and I told her he was also a friend of my daughter.

"I'd be glad to speak with you about Maureen if you think it would help. Unfortunately, I'm leaving for a three-day seminar in Boston today, so we can't get together until next week." She paused. "Unless you want to talk now on the phone."

Time was important, but so much more information comes out in person.

"I'll wait till you return. How's Tuesday?"

"I have a luncheon meeting at noon, but I'm free before that. Why don't you come here around ten," she suggested. "That should give us plenty of time."

I no sooner clicked off my call when Abby paraded through the doorway. The dogs, who had been sleeping by the table, dashed to greet her.

"I have some time before work, so I thought I'd stop by and find out what's going on. I'd also love an English muffin. Do you have any?"

"Of course."

As she popped a muffin into the toaster oven, I filled her in on what had happened. I asked if she wanted to visit Declan's aunt with me on Tuesday. I knew she was working this weekend and would have Tuesday off. She agreed to go.

"Afterwards, we could head up to Tarrytown and find out what we can about Austin Wells."

Abby nodded. "I've been thinking about Austin's pyramid scam. I wonder if he's been involved in this before."

"It's possible. Let's see what we can discover." I logged into my laptop and put the words *pyramid scams* into my search engine. Links to dozens of articles appeared. I pulled up one of the news stories.

"This involves a pyramid scam one year ago that operated in Baltimore," I said.

Abby came and stood behind my chair, leaning over me. As I scrolled down, a photo of the con artist appeared—it wasn't Austin.

"He looks more like the head of a tech start-up company." Abby chuckled.

"If a con artist looked like a con artist, no one would fall for the con," I reminded her.

"Try another article."

The next story didn't include a photo, but it did state that the schemer had two prior arrests—one in 2005 and the other in 1991.

"Austin appears to be in his forties," Abby said. "In 1991, he would have been a child."

I sat back and sighed. "This could take forever."

"Why don't you narrow the search?"

"Good idea. Austin has a home in Tarrytown. I'll look up pyramid scams that took place in locations within a day trip from that community."

"You might also narrow it to those scams that occurred more than two years ago. He probably would want to wait a bit before starting up again."

After several unsuccessful searches, I finally pulled up a news story on a pyramid scam in northern Connecticut seven years ago. I lucked out. On my screen was a picture of Austin Wells. He was identified in the story as Austin Jeffries.

I quickly read the article. This scam involved selling franchises for beauty products—for humans, not animals.

"It makes sense it would involve a different type of merchandise than what he's touting now," Abby said. "It lessens the chance of a connection."

The article went on to say Austin had disappeared and left his investors in the lurch before law enforcement could take any action.

The article gave a phone number for the police department in the town where this occurred.

I grabbed my phone and called the number. After a slight runaround, I was finally transferred to the Chief of Police. I told him why I was calling. I also asked him if he would be okay with me putting this on speaker, so my daughter could listen. He agreed.

"Austin Jeffries caused a lot of pain in this community," he said, after we'd gone over details of the scam. "We had one lady who died from a heart attack less than a month after he vanished. I believe it was brought about from the stress."

"Because of an investment of eight thousand dollars?" I asked.

"Yup. She only had her social security. Her brother, who lived about two hours away, helped out by giving her a few extra hundred every month. She told everyone it made a big difference, but she wanted to be independent. She saw the investment opportunity as a chance to do this."

"Where did she get the money to invest?"

"Her brother. She lied and told him she needed $8,000 for dental work. She planned to pay him back out of her commissions."

"And, of course, there were no commissions. Did her brother find out what she was doing?"

"Yup. They had a huge fight, and he stopped giving her

money. Without that monthly gift, she couldn't pay her rent. No one knows for sure what caused the heart attack, but most people in town feel it came from the stress."

I told the police chief about Austin Wells and how Austin Jeffries, based on the picture in a news article, was the same man.

"The news story says you were about to arrest him when he disappeared. Perhaps you can contact our local police and arrange to extradite him," I said.

He sighed. "I wish I could. But this happened almost seven years ago. The statute of limitations in this state for this particular crime is six years."

When the call was finished, Abby shook her head. "We better catch him before he vanishes again."

CHAPTER 33

Later that afternoon, I dressed for the Happy Place Animal Sanctuary's fundraiser. It was a casual affair so I donned white sandals and a sundress in shades of green and blue.

The fund raiser was a wine and cheese garden party being held on the lawn behind the sanctuary's administration building. When I arrived, I trekked up the path from the parking lot, listening to chirping crickets at dusk. As I came closer to the party location, that sound was replaced by the chatter of human conversation.

I headed to the bar which had been set up under a massive oak tree. I grabbed a white wine and stood quietly for a moment, sipping my drink and inhaling the evening scent of honeysuckle and pine. Then I spotted Lee Adler.

Lee was accompanied by a tall lady who sported a deep summer tan that contrasted with her short ash blond hair. He introduced us. Her name was Sabrina Stone. I admired the embroidered purse she carried, which she told me she bought at a small boutique earlier this summer when she and Lee spent a weekend in Montauk.

We were still making small talk when my phone trilled. I normally put it on silent mode when I'm at events, but tonight I kept it on in case Clara called with news about Olivia.

"Excuse me." I fished in my tote bag and grabbed the phone.

Spam. I stuffed it back in my tote.

"That's quite a bag," Sabrina said, grinning. "It's about the size of a small child."

I laughed. "I keep my life in here."

"Be careful. It's not good for your back." Sabrina paused. "I'm a chiropractor. I've had several patients who have suffered pain caused by carrying a big bag over time."

An idea flashed through my mind. This woman might be a good source of information about Lee.

"Sometimes I have knots in my neck," I said, which was true. "I know this is caused by tension, but I've been thinking about visiting a chiropractor."

Truth be told, I had thought about it but never got around to doing anything.

"Do you have a chiropractor?"

"No." I shook my head. "That's the problem."

She smiled, reached into her small clutch bag, and handed me a business card. "I'd be happy to help."

"I'm guessing you book far in advance."

"Not that far. I get a lot of emergencies. I also get cancellations. This afternoon, I received a call from one of my regulars canceling his appointment for tomorrow. It was for ten o'clock."

"If it's still available, I'll take it."

"Fine. See you then." She asked if Farrell was spelled with two Ls and then entered my name on her phone calendar.

Lee didn't look pleased, but all he said was, "Gina wants me to mingle with the guests. Will you excuse us?"

Lee and Sabrina headed toward a matronly-looking woman who was lingering near a table laden with assorted cheeses and fruits.

I spotted Gina only a few feet from where I stood. She was talking to a woman who was slightly overweight with frizzy strawberry blond hair and a bad sunburn. I made my way to them.

"This is Jessica James," Gina said. "She's my BFF."

"Call me Jessie."

"Jesse James? Really?

"My parents had a weird sense of humor. But it's spelled with an 'i' which is different than the outlaw."

"Jessie and I grew up together," Gina added.

Jessie nodded, "That's right. When we were kids we lived next door to each other on Long Island. When Gina moved, we still kept contact."

"We phoned each other all the time."

"Sharing our teenage angst," Jessie said.

"Do you still live on Long Island?" I asked Jessie.

"Yes. I own the *Book Nook*—that's the bookstore down the block from Harper University."

I filed that information in the back of my mind in case I needed to get in touch with Jessie. She and Gina were friends both before and after the disbarment of Gina's dad. What do best friends do? They confide in each other. They know each other's secrets.

Before I could make a comment, Gina said, "Excuse me. One of my biggest donors just arrived with his wife. I need to greet them."

"I know you're busy," Jessie said to Gina. "If I don't talk to you before I leave, I'll see you Sunday at the horse show."

"Are you a rider too?" I asked Jessie as Gina made her way across the lawn.

"No. But I occasionally go to the shows to cheer Gina on."

"I knew Gina rode, but I didn't know she competed."

"She's very good at it. Gina has a way with animals."

"I've heard she has a dog too."

"Her golden retriever and mine are both from the same litter, but hers is so much better behaved."

Jessie's comment put me on alert, but I didn't know why.

"I left my bottom dresser drawer open earlier today, and my dog grabbed a ball of rolled up socks and ran around the house with it," Jessie added. "I chased him for nearly ten minutes. He wouldn't come when I called. Gina's dog always obeys commands."

Now I knew what perked my interest. Detective Fox told me that Gina claimed her neighbor, who walked with a cane, couldn't chase after her dog when the dog escaped from the backyard.

But if the dog was trained to come when called, the neighbor wouldn't have to chase him. He would obey a command.

On the morning of Maureen's murder, did Gina really leave the sanctuary and go back to her house to rescue her dog?

Or did she go somewhere else in the sanctuary?

CHAPTER 34

I stepped into the chiropractic office with trepidation.

I'd never received a chiropractic adjustment although several of my friends swore by them. The main reason for this appointment was that I knew little about Lee Adler. I thought his girlfriend, Dr. Sabrina Stone, might be a good source of information.

Maybe Lee had no motive to kill Maureen, but I had to do due diligence and make sure. And I really did have knots in my neck.

At the reception desk, a young woman with long straight hair, the color of winter wheat, handed me a clipboard with a form. After filling it out, I was called into a treatment room and told to lay face down on the table. Dr. Sabrina Stone stepped inside, greeted me, and asked a few health-related questions. As she pressed down on my upper back, we began talking.

"How did you and Lee meet?" I asked.

"When I was in chiropractic college, I worked part-time for his parent's jewelry business. Lee was attending Harper University at the time, and he worked at the business part-time too." "So, you've known him for a while."

"Yes, but we didn't date until much later." Sabrina put pressure on the left side of my neck and I flinched.

"You definitely have knots," she said.

She went on with her story of how she and Lee first got together. "About two years after his parent's business closed, we ran into each other at a local coffee shop. We started talking, one thing led to another, and he asked me out. We've been together ever since."

As she continued adjusting me, she said, "Lee told me he had been through a bad period. He had no job and was forced to drop out of college because he couldn't pay the tuition. But now, things were looking up. He was working at the sanctuary and had gone back to school."

"I'm glad he's back at college part-time," I said.

"Oh, it's not part-time—he's full time now. Lee's a workaholic. He has a full-time job at the sanctuary, and he's in college full time. Most of his courses are at night, but one is in the day. Gina gives him time off for that."

I remembered Lee never said he was a part-time student. Since he worked full-time, I only assumed he was taking one or two courses. I now recalled his saying that Gina was flexible with his schedule.

"Attending school full-time must be costly," I said.

"Being a full-time student is to his advantage when it comes to money problems. His advisor helped him obtain a scholarship only available to full-time students. He saw Lee through a dark time when the tax fraud scandal first came to light."

"Sounds like a good advisor. What's his name?"

"Professor Philip Munch. Why?"

I ignored her questions and asked, "How does Lee get along with his parents after what happened? Is he angry with them?"

"At first he was angry, but when he realized they knew nothing about the tax fraud, he repaired his relationship and became supportive—especially once he realized how much they suffered too. They lost their business."

"His parents knew nothing of the tax fraud?"

"That's why they were never charged. The fraud was committed by their partner, David Link."

I heard the sound of my neck pop.

"All finished. You can get up now."

I got down from the table. I felt the tension gone from my neck.

"How can someone be a business partner and not be aware of what's going on in the business?" I asked.

"David Link was clever. He was a math whiz. Lee told me David cooked the books, but it never would have been discovered if it wasn't for the divorce."

"Divorce? What divorce?"

"David Link and his wife were in the midst of a divorce. His wife's lawyer hired a forensic accountant to review the company books and make sure he wasn't hiding any assets. Boy! Did she open a Pandora's Box! The forensic accountant uncovered tax fraud."

"Who was the divorce attorney?"

"I don't think Lee ever said." Sabrina shook her head.

I'd need to check, but I was sure the name would turn out to be Maureen McDermott.

* * * * *

On my way home, Abby called.

I told her about my conversation with Dr. Sabrina Stone.

There was silence. Finally, Abby spoke. "I know you're digging deep into the lives of all the suspects trying to ferret out motives. But even if you find strong motives, it won't prove who committed the crime. You need to tackle alibis."

"I may have a start on that." I told her about my conversation at the fund raiser with Gina's friend, who told me about Gina's well-trained dog. "Gina may not have been where she claimed to be."

"But you still can't prove where she was."

My daughter was right. As of now, there was no evidence putting any of the five suspects near the scene of the crime.

With the expansive sanctuary and set staff routine, each suspect would be away from each other for most of the time. This meant there was no way to verify alibis.

Was this case unsolvable?

CHAPTER 35

Horse shows start early. When I arrived at the fairgrounds a little after dawn on Sunday, the place was busier than a beehive. Horses were being led off trailers, grooms with brushes and curry combs were ensuring the animals looked their best, and a few riders were practicing in the rings.

I still had unanswered questions about Gina, especially in regards to her alibi. I also wondered when she found out Maureen McDermott was responsible for her father's disbarment. Gina was only a child when this took place. I was willing to bet Gina didn't discover the whole story until her father's memorial service when her mother came face to face with Maureen.

Although Gina would be too busy to talk until after her riding competition, her friend Jessie would be here. She might be able to fill in some gaps.

I surveyed my surroundings. I didn't spot Gina, but I spied Jessie on the end of a food truck line.

"I don't function this early," she said, smiling when I approached. "I need my caffeine."

"Me too."

After grabbing our coffees, we wandered off to a nearby bench and plopped ourselves down.

"Show starts at eight. Gina's group is one of the first to compete," Jessie said. "She's with her horse and a groom now."

"I'm interested in what you said the other day about your dog and Gina's dog. I find it fascinating that two dogs from the same litter behave so differently." This wasn't true. Individual personalities plus training made all the difference, but my comment was a good segue into the topic I wanted to explore.

"I was lax in training," Jessie responded.

"Did Gina train her dog herself, or did she hire a trainer?"

"She had a trainer when he was a little pup. When he grew older, she hired a handler."

"A handler?"

"Her McDuff is a retired show dog. He's won tons of blue ribbons."

Despite two veterinarians in my family, I didn't know much about the world of dog shows, but I imagined a good show dog would obey commands. Why wouldn't the neighbor call the dog to come? He wouldn't need to chase after it.

Jessie glanced at her watch. "I want to be sure I'm on time for Gina's competition. She likes having an audience."

"Does Gina's husband ever come to these events?" I asked, realizing he might be a source of information.

Jessie shook her head as a wicked smile spread across her face. "Never. She lucked out on that."

"What do you mean?"

"Nothing. You know how husbands are." Jessie's eyes widened. I'd seen that look before. It was as if she suddenly remembered I was a reporter.

She had said too much.

Jessie turned her head. "I spot an old friend that I haven't seen in ages. I have to go." Jessie took off, and I remained on the bench, sipping my coffee and thinking about Jessie's statement. "She lucked out" was an odd comment, but was it important? I was curious about what she said but more curious as to why she appeared to regret saying it.

I continued sipping my coffee until I spotted Sam Garcia leading a horse to a water trough. I remembered he still worked part-time with horses.

I hurried over to him. If he was surprised to see me, he didn't show it.

After an initial chat about horses, I got to the question I'd been burning to ask.

"Sam, why didn't you tell me that Maureen McDermott was responsible for your father's restaurant closing?"

He hesitated. "Why do you think? I was afraid I'd look guilty."

"You claim you're happier working with animals than in the restaurant business, but your father lost everything."

"I know. I was so angry with Maureen. But I didn't kill her. I believe in karma. She was a miserable person, and I believe miserable people live in a world of unhappiness."

The horse finished drinking and shook its head. The water surrounding its mouth sprayed in my direction. I wiped it off with my arm.

"I need to go," Sam said. He took off, leading the horse toward a grassy area.

I wandered for a bit and watched several competitions, including Gina's for which she placed first. I figured she'd be in a good mood, so now would be a perfect time to talk. I found her brushing her horse.

"Congratulations," I said.

"Thanks." She stopped brushing her horse and eyed me suspiciously. "What brings you here?'

"My daughter competed when she was younger," I said, flashing back to Abby's teen years. "I haven't been to a horse show in a while, so when Jessie mentioned you were competing today, I thought I'd watch."

Gina still appeared wary.

I paused. "I also have a question to ask."

"I'm not surprised." She didn't seem pleased.

"Your dog is a show dog. Why did you need to go home when he escaped? Why didn't your neighbor just command him to come? Surely, he was trained to respond. No one would need to chase him."

"Because my neighbor is scared to death of dogs—all dogs, including my sweet and well-trained McDuff. There is no way he would call to the dog and have McDuff bound toward him."

I nodded. There were people like this. People terrified of dogs. I realized this was possible.

Then she added, "The video cameras at the sanctuary gate cover both the entrance and the exit. The tapes can provide a record of when I departed and returned to the sanctuary. So can the security guard who waved to me when I left and when I re-entered. I assume that's why you're interested."

I groaned. Of course. She couldn't lie about this. The security cameras would have a record. Another theory down the drain.

I quickly changed the subject. "I thought your husband might be here cheering you on."

A flicker of fear flashed in her eyes. "No. He's too busy, and he's not into horses." She added, impatiently, "I need to get by where you're standing."

I knew I'd get no more from her today, so I said goodbye and left. I was making my way to the food truck to buy another cup of coffee when I heard my name.

"Kristy Farrell, yoo-hoo!"

I spun around. Coming toward me was a large woman dressed entirely in pink—hot pink Capris, deep pink shirt, and open toed pink sandals.

Open toed pink sandals! At a horse show! What was she thinking?

I hoped she watched where she walked.

"Alicia Layne," I called. "I haven't seen you in months."

Alicia Layne, who was in her late fifties, tended to stand out in a crowd. She taught drama at a local college, and also acted in summer stock theatre. I remembered her performance as Madame Arcadi from Noel Coward's *Blithe Spirit*—a role that suited her perfectly. Back when I taught English, I brought her to the high school as a guest lecturer, and we became friends.

"What are you doing here?" I asked.

"I have a role in a British mystery. My character is an upper crust Englishwoman whose life revolves around riding, which I know nothing about." She threw open her arms like wings of a giant bird. "So I came here to immerse myself in the proper atmosphere."

"Do you need to ride a horse or be near one on stage?" I asked. I didn't think so, but with Alicia, one never knew for sure.

"Of course not. But I need to understand my character's feelings and emotions."

I smiled. When Alicia had a role, she wanted to experience it.

"Why are you here?" she asked me.

"Someone I know is competing today."

"Who?" Alicia could be blunt.

"Gina Garone."

"Oh, Gina. I know her too."

"You do?"

"She and her husband are big contributors to a community theatre program that is dear to my heart."

"I knew she was involved in animal and environmental causes, but I didn't know about her work with the arts."

"The Garones are involved with everything. Generous people." She glanced at her watch. "I need to scoot. I'm meeting a trainer who is going to explain this whole horse show thing to me."

In addition to being a good actress, Alicia Layne was good at something else—gossiping. If she knew the Garones, chances are she would know if Gina and her husband had issues. Although Gina's home life probably had no connection to the sanctuary murder, I still needed more information on Gina—her social media only presented what she wanted others to see.

"Why don't we get together for lunch this week?" I asked Alicia.

"I'd love to get together. But I have a better idea than lunch."

She told me her idea. I rolled my eyes but agreed.

We set a time and place to meet tomorrow. After Alicia departed, I wandered through the fairgrounds. It was only ten o'clock. I was going to leave and head to church when I came across Sam Garcia again. He was standing next to a picnic table near one of the food trucks. His back was to me, and he was on his cell phone.

"She had to pay for what she did," he said into the phone. "We'll talk later. Good-bye."

He laid his phone on the table, then spun around, spotted me, and scowled.

"Were you talking about Maureen McDermott?" I accused him.

"No. Not that it's any of your business. I was talking to my mother about my sister."

I stood silently, my arms folded in front.

He stared at me, defiantly.

"My younger sister got her driver's license less than a month ago," he said. "She backed into my mother's car. They both have high deductibles, and since the damage wasn't extensive, they decided not to report it. My sister was afraid it would affect her insurance premiums."

He rubbed his hands across his face. "Anita, that's my sister, caused the accident. She was texting while driving. I told her she had to pay for repairing both cars. She did, but my mother feels guilty. She said Anita doesn't have a lot of money."

"She had to pay for what she did," I repeated the phrase he used on the phone. "You were talking about your sister."

He nodded. I wasn't sure I believed him, but before I could say anything, someone yelled, "Horse loose. In the left field."

Sam raced off in the direction of the cry for help. In his rush, he forgot his phone. It was still on the picnic table.

I didn't think it should be left here, so I grabbed it. I'd wait until the horse was back where it belonged, and then I'd seek out Sam and return the device.

I decided to check recent calls. The last one was listed as *Mom,* so I guessed what he said was true. But being a curious sort—my daughter calls it nosy—I scrolled further down.

I gasped. I didn't believe what I saw.

At that moment Sam was heading toward me.

"Thanks," he said as he grabbed the phone from me.

"I need to ask—"

"Not now," he interrupted. "I have to get back to work."

"Sam, we need you right now," a voice called from about thirty feet away.

"I'm coming."

"I'll talk to you later this week," I said as he turned and began rushing toward the direction of the voice. What we needed to discuss would probably require more than a few minutes. It had to do with what I saw on his phone.

On the day of the murder, he received a call at five-thirty in the morning. It was from Maureen McDermott.

CHAPTER 36

The next morning, the jarring trill of my phone woke me. Clara's name popped up.

"Is it Olivia?" I held my breath. "Is she out of the coma?"

"No. And no one appears to know when—or if—that will happen. I'm calling because corporate is sending us a temporary editor in her absence."

"It's seven-fifteen in the morning. Couldn't this message have waited?" Clara knew I was not a morning person. It takes me time to become coherent.

"I wanted to be sure I reached you with this message. Our new editor called me at home at seven this morning. He told me to notify all employees that he's coming tomorrow, and he's calling a staff meeting for four o'clock."

As I stretched, I realized my schedule for tomorrow was chocked full. I hadn't planned on going into the office.

As if knowing what I was thinking, Clara said, "It's a *must attend* meeting."

* * * * *

"I don't want to mislead you." Alicia Layne said. She sat across from me, sipping her tea.

Alicia had decided that instead of meeting for lunch, we

145

should go for high tea—more immersion into English life for her role in a British mystery. After spending the morning working at home, I was now at the Ivy Bridge Tea Room.

"How could you mislead me?" I asked. A harpist played nearby, but the music was soft enough that conversation could be heard.

"I don't know the Garones as well as you may think I do," Alicia answered. "We served on a fundraising committee to introduce inner city children to the theatre. Everyone puts their best foot forward at committee meetings."

"Still, as an actress, you have excellent insight into people." I hoped a little flattery might convince her to talk.

It worked.

"Well, I did get to see more of her since I started prepping for my role," she said, after wiping clotted cream from her chin. "This weekend's horse show wasn't my first. I've been to three others where Gina competed. And I was at a party on their estate a month ago."

"What are the Garones like?"

"Rich." She smiled. "And generous. Frank Garone has lots of money and would give his wife anything she wanted whether it's jewelry, a thoroughbred horse, or a job."

We both sipped our tea. I wished mine was coffee, but I had to admit this tea was delicious.

Alicia placed her cup back on her saucer as she continued talking. "Gina did a lot of volunteer work. But with her son away at boarding school, she felt she wanted more. She wanted to be in charge of something. When her friend Carolyn Whitcome mentioned plans to establish an animal sanctuary, Gina wanted to be director."

"I heard her husband donated the money to buy the land."

"He basically bought her the job. No one ever said it, but I believe the deal was '*no job, no land*,'"

I nodded. That was what I'd heard too.

Alicia grabbed a scone. I think it was her fourth. "But Gina is good at the job," she said. "She has rich friends. She's a fabulous fundraiser."

"But running a sanctuary involves more than fundraising," I argued.

Alicia shrugged. "She hired a competent business manager. Believe me, her role as a fundraiser is far more important than bean counting."

Running an institution such as a sanctuary required a little more skill than bean counting. But I decided to ignore that for the present and take another track.

"I noticed her husband wasn't at the horse show," I said. "Does he support her competitive riding?"

"He is *money* supportive. He gives her anything she wants, but they don't spend a great deal of time together. I also heard he doesn't want to spend his Sundays at horse shows. He prefers golfing at his country club."

"Did she marry for money?"

Alicia bit into her scone and finished chewing. "I think money played a part, but I honestly think Gina is fond of him, and he loves her."

Alicia winked. "They definitely are not Romeo and Juliet. In some ways, their marriage reminds me of King Arthur, Guinevere, and Lancelot."

I almost spilled my tea. Guinevere was King Arthur's wife and queen. Lancelot was her lover.

I thought of asking Alicia exactly what she meant, but her explanations tended to be convoluted and far-fetched.

I simply said, "Did Gina have an affair?"

"I heard she strayed. But only once. I heard she felt guilty."

I wondered. Guilty at the affair or afraid of ruining a lucrative marriage? I didn't know Gina well enough to tell.

"Do you know who her lover was?"

Alicia nodded. "One of the part time stable hands. He's so handsome too." She winked again. "A real hunk."

"Do you know his name?"

"I believe his name was Sam." She smiled mischievously and winked. "And I heard he also works at the animal sanctuary."

CHAPTER 37

The next morning, I picked up Abby, entered Regina Carr's address into my car's navigational system, and we took off on our journey.

"Does she know the trouble Declan is in?" Abby asked.

"I'm not sure what she knows. She's aware he's a suspect, but I can't tell if she realizes that he's the number one suspect."

I shook my head and continued. "Declan claims they're not close. Declan says his schedule and his aunt's schedule made it difficult to get together. But I have a feeling she keeps tabs on him."

We arrived at our destination. Scarsdale was an upscale suburb north of Manhattan. Regina Carr lived on a tree-lined street of Colonial style homes set back from the road. I pulled into her circular driveway.

Regina greeted us at the door wearing a light blue linen suit. I remembered she would be going to a luncheon meeting after we finished our conversation.

"How did you know Maureen McDermott?" I asked after we were seated in the living room, and Declan's aunt had served us coffee in fine china cups.

"We butted heads on a few cases."

"So, you weren't friends." I grinned.

"I don't think she had any friends. But no. We most definitely

149

were not."

I arched an eyebrow. "You seem emphatic about that."

"I'm friends with lots of attorneys who oppose me in court. But Maureen was different. She was vengeful and vindictive."

"How?"

"She would bad mouth opposing attorneys out of court. Try to smear their reputations."

"Did she do that to you?"

"She tried. And it got worse after I opposed her nomination for a judgeship."

Whoa! "What happened?" I asked.

"I was active in the bar association. Maureen's name had been proposed by one of the political parties for a judgeship in the family court. I think she helped one of the bigwigs get a good divorce settlement."

Regina hesitated. "I didn't think Maureen had the temperament for a judgeship. I also felt several of her past actions were unethical. I convinced the judicial committee of the bar association not to endorse her. Her political party didn't want to run her without the bar association backing."

"So she didn't become a judge, and she blamed you."

"Maureen always blamed others when she didn't get what she wanted. But yes, she blamed me."

We finished our coffee and said good-bye. As we pulled out of Regina Carr's driveway and headed toward Tarrytown, I said to Abby, "Now we know why Maureen had it out for Declan."

Abby nodded. "His aunt destroyed Maureen McDermott's dream."

CHAPTER 38

After leaving Regina Carr, we sped off to Tarrytown, a picturesque village, famous as the home of author Washington Irving. On the way, I told Abby about my conversation with Alicia Layne and what Alicia told me about a fling between Gina and someone named Sam.

"Sam Garcia?"

I nodded.

"What if Maureen found out and blackmailed Gina," Abby theorized. "Blackmail is a motive for murder."

"I agree. It's possible."

Abby and I continued discussing the murder. In a short while, I spotted the sign for Tarrytown.

"We should be there in a few minutes," I said.

"Do you think the Ajax Pet Products factory really exists?" Abby asked. Our topic changed from Maureen McDermott's demise to the pyramid scheme.

"I'm pretty sure. Austin let it slip in conversation that he lives in Tarrytown. My instinct tells me the factory would be near where he lives."

"If it's here, how do you expect to find it?"

"This isn't a huge community, and we're searching for a factory. That type of building tends to stand out. We'll ask questions. Someone is bound to have heard of it."

Abby shook her head. "This is a long shot."

I grinned. "I also snapped photos of Austin Wells and his cohort, Mille Topper, at the dinner. Maybe someone will recognize the photos. There's a gas station up ahead. Let's stop. We're only a mile from the village."

We pulled into the service station. While Abby topped off my tank, I made my way to the office.

Two elderly men were seated playing checkers. One was bald with a bushy gray beard. The other had bushy gray hair and no beard.

"I'm looking for the Ajax Pet Products factory," I said. "Can you tell me how to get there?"

The bald man raised his finger, signaling me to wait. He moved his black checker and collected a red one. Then he said to me, "Got an address?"

"I'm afraid not. I thought you might be able to tell me where it is."

"Never heard of it. Have you, Artie?"

The other man didn't speak—he appeared deep in thought. He moved his red checker. "Nope. I never heard of it either."

"Thanks anyway." I departed the office. When Abby finished with the gasoline, we drove until we entered the village of Tarrytown.

"Now what?" she asked.

"Let's find a place for lunch. Perhaps the wait staff will be familiar with Ajax."

We located a coffee shop in the center of town. We both ordered the lunch special—tomato soup and grilled cheese.

The server was an overweight, middle-aged woman with short white hair and a jolly face. She reminded me of Mrs. Santa Claus, except for the skull tattoo on her left arm. I asked if she knew of the Ajax factory.

She shook her head. "I've lived in Tarrytown my entire life, and I've never heard of it."

I pulled out my phone and scrolled to the pictures I'd taken at the Ajax dinner and sales meeting. "Do you recognize either of these people?"

She squinted at the photos. I knew they weren't great shots.

"That's Austin and Mille Briggs," she said. "When they're in town, sometimes they come here for dinner. They also order meals to go."

So, Austin Wells and Miller Topper were Austin and Mille Briggs. If they ordered meals to go that meant someone at this restaurant had their address.

"Do you know if they're home now?"

"He was here last week for a few days—alone. He came in for dinner, and when he left, he said he'd be back in a few weeks. Don't know much about them. They seem to travel a lot."

"I need to contact them. They won $1,000 in a contest," I lied. "I want to leave a note in their mailbox, but, unfortunately, I lost their address."

"No problem. I'll get it."

She brought us the address along with our soups and sandwiches.

"Someone probably takes in their mail," she said. "They're often gone for weeks on end."

We ate quickly and headed out to find the home of Austin and Millie Briggs.

"What are you planning to do, Mom?"

"I'm not sure. The server at the restaurant said she never heard of Ajax. In a small community, someone who lived here a long time would know if such a factory existed. I'm thinking maybe the factory is a manufacturing operation they run out of a house."

"But if Austin's not here, how can we find out? We can't trespass."

"Can't we?" I smiled.

We drove. As we turned onto the block where the Briggses lived, a delivery truck passed us by. Upon arriving at the house, I noticed a package on the front porch.

"Let's see what that is." I hopped out of the car. Abby followed.

We made it to the front porch when a voice called out, "May I help you?"

A woman wearing shorts, a halter top, and flip-flops, cut across the lawn and climbed the three steps to the porch. I judged her age to be mid-twenties.

"We're looking for the Briggses," I said.

"They're not here. I take in the mail and other deliveries when they're gone. Don't want to leave them here for package trolls." She eyed us suspiciously.

She grabbed the package, but not before I had the chance to see the return address.

It came from Omega Animal Grooming Supplies.

"Do you think the Omega Corporation is involved in the Ajax scam?" Abby asked once we left the Briggs house and began our journey home.

"Yes, but they don't know it. Omega is a victim too. At least, I think it is."

"A victim? Do you want to explain?"

I shook my head. "Not until I'm sure. Or at least pretty sure."

"How can you find out?"

"I need you to do me a favor. Call Teresa Lamonica and ask if you can get a sample of their dog shampoo."

"Okay. But why?"

'I need to have it chemically analyzed."

CHAPTER 39

Nick Lamonica hopped out of an old beat-up Honda. He was the reason I was at the sanctuary early today. Nick was taking me on a tour of the food storage facility. I intended to include information on this in my magazine story.

"We need to drive there. It's at the north end of the property." He pointed to an old pick-up truck with the words *Happy Place Animal Sanctuary* painted on the side. "C'mon."

I jumped into the front passenger seat while he took the driver's spot and started the engine. Off we went. The path was not paved, and it was a bumpy ride.

"It seems to be away from everything, including the animals," I said as I jumped out of the truck once we reached our destination. "Isn't it inconvenient?"

"Not at all. First thing in the morning, the animal keepers load the food they need onto one of our pick-up trucks. Then we drive off and feed the animals in our care. We only go here once a day."

Nick swung open the door to the long cement building, and we stepped inside.

"We keep mostly grains and food pellets in this part," he said as my gaze swept the room, noting the barrels, boxes, and crates sitting on raised platforms. "The rest of our food—meats, fish, and vegetables—we keep in the refrigerated section."

I followed Nick to the back where I spotted a sign marked *Refrigeration*. Nick unlatched the door.

Brrr. I felt the cold air before we entered. Inside this cavernous area were crates of vegetables plus large sections containing meat and seafood.

Nick grabbed a cart, and I followed him.

"Give me a few minutes to load up. Then I'll take you on our feeding rounds." He grinned as he looked at me shivering. "If you want, you can wait outside this room where it's warmer."

I did want.

"See you outside," I said, grinning. As I turned, I spotted Sam Garcia hauling a cart loaded with carrots. He was headed toward the exit too.

"Sam," I called. I dashed toward him. "Do you have a minute?"

He turned. "Not really. I'm busy." He continued on his way.

I needed to question him about what I'd seen on his phone the other day at the horse show. Ignoring his attempt to brush me off, I zoomed straight to the point. "Maureen called you at five-thirty in the morning on the day of her murder. Why?"

"How do you know that?" Suddenly his puzzled expression transformed to anger. He glared at me. "Oh, you looked at my phone, right?"

"Sorry, but a woman was murdered. If you didn't do it, don't you want the real killer to be found? Otherwise, you'll always be considered a suspect."

Before he reacted, I added, "If I knew what was so urgent that morning, it might help."

"Maureen wanted me to work with her later in the morning organizing supplies." He shook his head. "As a part-time keeper back then, I only worked half a day. Because of that, I didn't have as many animals under my care as the full-time keepers, but I was expected to assist the others if they had projects. Maureen always did have something she wanted me to do."

"But why did she call so early? Couldn't she wait until you arrived at work?"

Sam frowned. "That was how she operated. She was an early riser, and she didn't care if she inconvenienced anyone else. In fact, she took pleasure in being annoying. I think it gave her a sense of power. I have to go now."

Sam left and in a few moments Nick appeared. "Are you ready to feed the animals?"

After loading the back of the truck, we took off. Since Nick was responsible for the large animals, he showed me the safety precautions he used in feeding dangerous predators, such as the bear and the wolves, and how the food was hidden so the animals had to forage as they would in the wild. I also learned of animal eating habits that I hadn't known.

"I never realized bears liked peaches so much," I said. "I've always pictured them with salmon in their mouths."

"Bears love sweets too."

I smiled as I remembered my favorite storybook bear and his honeypot.

When we finished, I asked Nick to drop me off at the administration building. I had a few questions for Gina that I needed answered before I could complete my feature story.

When I stepped into the building, Wendy was behind the reception desk. She was staring down at her desk, a frown spread across her face.

"Good morning," I said.

She jumped. "You startled me. I didn't see you come in."

I noticed an open notebook on her desk and wondered if something written in it was causing her to frown. Wendy must have noticed me looking, because she immediately stashed it in a drawer.

"I've two quick questions for Gina," I said. "Could I see her for a moment?"

"She's not here. She's meeting with a potential donor." Wendy twisted her necklace. "Gina spends more time away from the office than in it."

"Cultivating donors is a big part of her job," I said.

"Yes. But it's not the only thing. She should be more hands-on here."

"What do you mean?"

"It's complicated."

I wondered if she thought she'd said too much, because she avoided my eyes and spoke no more on the topic.

"Do you want to make an appointment to speak with Gina?" she asked in a businesslike tone.

We set up an interview time for tomorrow. I talked with Wendy for a few more minutes and mentioned that I'd just finished a tour of the storage facility with Nick.

As I turned to leave, Wendy asked, "Do you remember how many cartons of carrots you saw?"

"No. I don't."

I thought that was a strange question.

CHAPTER 40

As I glanced to my right, I saw it.

I was stopped at a traffic light when I spotted the *Book Nook* in a row of stores in a strip mall. This book shop was owned by Gina's friend Jessie James. Since I had a few minutes to spare, I pulled into an open parking spot. I still had unanswered questions about Gina, and instinct told me Jessie would have the answers.

Whether or not she would share the information with me was another matter.

A chime rang as I swung open the door and stepped inside. There were rows and rows of books. Each section was decorated with colorful posters according to genre—whimsical characters in the children's area, famous figures from the past in the history portion, and animals and flowers by the nature books. There was also a comfortable seating area with a coffee bar.

I maneuvered through the narrow aisles to the back of the room where Jessie was perched on a stool behind a counter next to the cash register. She was reading a book.

"Hi, Jessie." I said as I approached. "Do you have a moment?"

She looked up. "It depends. What do you want? A book?"

"Maybe later." I smiled. "Right now I have a question. When did Gina discover that Maureen McDermott was responsible for her father's disbarment?"

159

"Who?"

"Maureen McDermott. The animal keeper who was murdered at Happy Place Animal Sanctuary."

Maureen's death was a major news story on Long Island, where murder is a rarity. And it occurred at the sanctuary where her best friend Gina worked. There's no way Jessie didn't recognize Maureen's name.

"Now I remember who she was," Jessie replied.

"Was Gina told as a child about Maureen?"

"I don't think so."

"According to Gina, you phoned each other frequently after she moved from Sands Point to Wayside, New Jersey. Didn't she ever talk about what happened?"

"No. Gina was a young girl when her father lost his law license and her family moved. She didn't know many details."

"I heard that at the recent memorial service for Gina's dad, Mrs. Molinari recognized Maureen. Do you think that's when she told Gina?"

Jessie averted my eyes and didn't respond.

"You're her best friend. Gina would have told you once she found out," I added.

Jessie sighed. "Okay. Right after the memorial service, Gina's mom told her Maureen McDermott was the attorney responsible for her father's disbarment. Gina confided this to me later that day."

"How did Gina react?"

"She was shocked and angry." Jessie paused. "But she hasn't brought it up since then. Gina rarely talked about her past. I respect her privacy."

"Do you think—?"

"What are you up to?" Jessie narrowed her eyes. "You consider Gina a suspect, don't you? Why? Because the murdered woman may have been responsible for Gina's father's disbarment thirty years ago? That's crazy."

"There's possibly a more compelling motive," I said quietly. "Perhaps Maureen was blackmailing Gina."

"Blackmailing Gina? For what?"

"For having a fling with Sam Garcia."

Jessie flinched. The look in her eyes said she knew about it.

"The last thing Gina would want is for someone to destroy her lucrative marriage," I said.

"She didn't marry Frank for his money. Despite rumors, Gina loves her husband. She had an indiscretion with Sam but only once." Jessica shoulders sagged. "Gina's husband had been working non-stop on a project. Meanwhile, Gina was involved in competitive riding and saw Sam at horse shows as well as at the sanctuary. He was charming and a bit of a flirt."

"He's handsome," I admitted.

"Another rider spotted them behind the barn if you get my drift. This rider spread the story." Jessica paused. "But even if Maureen heard the rumor, she couldn't blackmail Gina."

"Why?"

"Because you can't threaten to tell a secret if it's not a secret. Gina found out that the story was being spread, so she decided to get out in front of it. Gina confessed to her husband. She told him it was only kissing, and it happened one time. This is all true."

"Did he forgive her?"

"Yes. He was upset, but he did forgive her. They're going for counseling."

The chime rang, signaling another visitor entering the store. I took that as a sign to leave. I wasn't going to get more information from Jessie today.

As I made my way back to the door, I passed an area decorated with posters featuring Sherlock Holmes and Agatha Christie—the mystery section. I glanced at my watch. I wanted to browse, but I didn't have the time. I think this was the first instance where I left a bookstore without buying a book.

But I had one more stop before my staff meeting—an important stop.

CHAPTER 41

My important stop was Harper University. I wanted to talk to Lee Adler's advisor, Professor Munch. My research showed that he finished his first class of the day at two o'clock, and his next one didn't start until four. I figured there was a good chance he'd be in his office in-between teaching.

When I arrived, he was with a student. I hadn't made an appointment because I didn't want to give him the opportunity to check me out. It was important to get the information I was seeking, so I wouldn't be entirely truthful about the reason for my visit.

I waited outside. After the student left, I poked my head inside his office.

"Good morning, Professor Munch," I said, cheerfully. "Could I see you for a moment?"

He glanced at his watch. "I have another student coming in ten minutes."

"Great. I only need five." I stepped into the office and slid into the chair across from his desk. "It's about Lee Adler."

"Lee? What about him?" Professor Munch ran his hand through his gray mustache.

"I work for *Animal Advocate Magazine*. I met Lee while researching a story on the Happy Place Animal Sanctuary." That was the truthful part of my undercover story.

I took a deep breath and continued, now stretching the truth. "We're looking to hire a new business manager, and I thought he might be a good fit for us. I know you're his advisor. I have only one quick question."

He scowled. "This is highly irregular. Most references are requested in writing."

"We're not asking for a reference now. And this is something that probably shouldn't be in writing."

His scowl deepened.

"It's important to know how a prospective employee acts during a crisis. How was he during his family's trouble with their jewelry business?"

Professor Munch, still frowning, sat back in his chair. I was afraid he wouldn't answer.

"Lee's a private person. He keeps to himself. He rarely said anything about the problem," the professor admitted.

"Was he angry, especially with his parents?" I waved my hand to shoo away an annoying fly. Professor Munch's window was wide open, and there was no screen.

"His parents weren't involved in the fraud. But he did confide in me that he thought they should have been more aware of the company's finances."

Professor Munch moved forward in his chair and formed a steeple with his hands. "Once, but only once, he expressed anger at his parents' business partner. I believe his name was David Link." The professor paused. "Lee handles himself well in crisis situations."

"What about the divorce lawyer responsible for uncovering the fraud? How did he feel about her?"

The professor stared at me with a blank expression on his face and shrugged as if he hadn't a clue as to what I meant.

"The attorney for David Link's spouse was the one who hired the forensic accountant. This attorney's name was Maureen

McDermott," I explained. "Was Lee angry with her?"

"He never mentioned her. Knowing Lee, he probably felt she was just doing her job."

I shooed the fly away again as I rose from my chair. "One more question. When does he complete his degree?"

"In one more year. If you hire him, you will accommodate his schedule, right?"

"Of course. It's great that he has a scholarship, so he can go here full-time."

"Oh, he doesn't have that scholarship anymore. Unfortunately, the alumnus who sponsored the scholarship passed away. His family chose not to continue."

"Too bad. I hate to see young people saddled with large loans."

"As far as I know, he's not applying for a loan. I believe the remaining tuition is coming out of his pocket."

Harper University was an expensive college. The salaries of all sanctuary staff were listed in the annual report. Considering what Lee was paid, I wondered how he could afford this.

Professor Munch must have read the expression on my face because he quickly added, "Lee is an excellent money manager."

"He must be." I was still standing next to the chair.

"If your magazine does hire him, it will be a big loss to the animal sanctuary. They'll need to hire a replacement immediately. From what Lee has told me, if the current director was left handling the day-to-day operations, the facility would have gone bankrupt."

I sat back down. I wasn't ready to leave. "What do you mean?"

"When Lee was first hired to work at the sanctuary, it was as a clerk. The director was handling all the business decisions— Lee was only doing the paperwork."

Professor Munch sat back and scratched his cheek near his mustache. "At one point, the sanctuary couldn't afford to pay its bills. That's when Lee stepped in and worked out a payment schedule. From that point on, the board chair insisted he take over all business operations and the director only handle marketing and fundraising. Lee discussed this with me because he wanted my advice about taking on the new responsibilities."

My mouth was open so wide the fly almost flew in.

The board chair, Carolyn Whitcome, was a good friend of the director, Gina Garone. For Carolyn to take power away from Gina, it had to be a dire situation. Poor financial management might mean the closing of the sanctuary. That would be a major black mark on Gina.

It appeared Carolyn, Lee, and Gina went to big efforts to keep this quiet.

I wondered if Maureen McDermott knew and threatened to make it public.

CHAPTER 42

I raced from the parking lot into the office.

Clara was not at her desk, and no one else was around. I realized everyone must be in the conference room for the meeting with the new editor.

I bee-lined into the conference room. All of the magazine's employees sat around the long table with worried or solemn expressions. We were a small staff. Aside from Clara, who was the administrative assistant, there was our editorial assistant, advertising director, art and photo director, production manager, and the senior reporter—I was the junior.

Standing at the far end head of the table was a man who appeared to be in his early thirties wearing a dark suit. The image of a viper flashed through my mind as I stared at his protruding jaw and heavy eyelids.

He had been speaking when I arrived and didn't look happy about the interruption. He glanced at his watch. "You're late."

The meeting was scheduled for four in the afternoon. It was one minute past four.

"I'm sorry. I was working on my story."

"This meeting is top priority. You should have adjusted your schedule."

I was taken aback. Olivia's top priority was always the story.

"It won't happen again." I slid into an empty chair between

Clara and the senior reporter.

"As I was saying," he continued. "My name is Griffin DeMott. I'll be your editor, at least temporarily."

He went on to fill us in on his background. He was a graduate of an Ivy League university with a business degree. He worked in the financial industry before joining the corporation that now owned *Animal Advocate*. He never mentioned any journalism experience.

"I will review all feature stories before they go to print." He went on to say, "I'll make sure they are appropriate."

"What does that mean?" I asked.

Judging by his frown, I probably should have kept my mouth shut, but he did reply, "I will make sure they do not offend any of our advertisers." He pointed to Grace, our advertising director. "Grace and I will work together on this."

I exchanged glances with my colleague, the senior reporter.

"What about the editor's column?" the senior reporter asked. "Olivia always wrote a column updating our readers on animal legislation and other issues."

"She prepared one for this issue before her accident," Clara answered, her voice quaking. "I have it on my computer."

"Good." Griffin nodded. "I'll check it, and if it is appropriate, we'll use it. After that, we'll probably discontinue the column. I certainly don't have time to write one."

Griffin paused and then said, "This brings me to my final point. I'm asking everyone in the room to bring in another advertiser."

"We're reporters, not sales staff," blurted out the senior reporter.

Griffin frowned again. "If you don't do this, you may not be a reporter for long. It's all about the bottom line. If we don't increase revenue, we will need to reduce expenses and that means layoffs."

He stared directly at the senior reporter and me. "We might wind up with only one reporter, and we would secure other stories from free-lancers. Our editorial assistant and administrative assistant jobs could be combined too."

He ended the meeting. I headed back to my cubicle in a despondent mood as I digested the implications of Griffin's comments. *Animal Advocate* currently included two articles from freelancers in each issue—the rest came from the senior reporter and me. The magazine would save money if they let me go and bought more freelance articles to cover the void.

Moments later, Clara came into my office. Her red eyes were a sign she had been crying.

"I need this job Kristy," she said. "When my husband died, he didn't have insurance. This is my only source of income."

"I'm sure Griffin will keep you on."

"I don't think so. When he talked about combining my job with Janet's editorial assistant position, I realized she's qualified to do my job, but I have no background in editorial work. It will be me who goes."

"His threat to downsize may be just that—a threat. He won't do it."

Clara and I stared at each other. We knew this statement wasn't true.

No sooner had Clara left when my phone trilled. It was Abby.

I talked to Teresa Lamonica," my daughter said. "She's dropping off samples of the dog shampoo at the veterinary office later today. We're open late, so it works out perfectly. She should be here soon."

"She's still in town?" Most conferences didn't last this long.

"She decided to take a few days off and vacation in the Hamptons after the conference ended. She's headed back home today, and she'll pass near the veterinary office on the way to the airport. She has the shampoo in her sample case."

"You better fill Dad in on what we're doing. I don't want him blindsided if he runs into her when she drops off the sample."

Abby laughed. "You're right. Teresa may think we're interested in buying the product and try to convince him. I know how much Dad hates sales pressure."

I ended the call and was about to leave when the intercom on my office phone rang.

"There's a call for you from a Wendy Wu," Clara said.

"Thanks. I'll take it." I connected with Wendy.

"I hope you don't mind my calling you at work?" Wendy said. "I didn't know how else to reach you."

"No problem. I should have given you my cell number. What's up?"

"I need to show you something. When will you be at the sanctuary?"

"I'll be there tomorrow. I'm meeting with Gina."

"Good. I'll be there from eight until one in the afternoon. But I don't want anyone to know we were speaking. Perhaps we could meet after I leave—but not in the office."

"Where then?"

"Let's meet by the fox exhibit a few minutes after one o'clock. The fox hides out during the day, so there's not much to see. That means there aren't a lot of people in the area."

"Can you tell me what this is about?"

Wendy hesitated. "I think it's better if you see what I have."

CHAPTER 43

After whipping around the house and picking up my husband's extraneous laundry and other out of place items, I locked the dogs and cat upstairs and vacuumed animal hair off the furniture. I get more cleaning done ten minutes before company arrives than during any other time.

As I began brewing a pot of coffee, Matt sauntered into the room. "When will everyone get here?"

"Momentarily." I glanced at my watch. "But I hope Abby and Jason come first. I want to talk with them before Austin arrives."

As on cue, Abby burst through the door, followed by Jason and a stranger.

"This is Detective Bill Cooper." Jason introduced us to his companion who was a big, burly man with growing stubble covering his cheeks and chin. Both Jason and Detective Cooper were dressed in jeans and tee shirts.

"Have you dug up any additional information on Austin or Ajax Pet Products since we last spoke?" I asked Jason.

"You were right," he said. "His real name is Austin Briggs, and Mille is his wife. They ran this pyramid scam before—not only in Connecticut but also in Pennsylvania and New Jersey. They only stay in an area for three to four months, then they lay low, and start up a year or two later in a new location."

"Last week was their third monthly dinner and sales meeting

on Long Island," Detective Cooper added, "so right now, they are probably tying up loose ends. There won't be a fourth dinner meeting. They'll disappear and leave their victims holding the bag."

"Unless we stop them tonight." Jason grinned.

The bell rang. While Matt headed to the door, I whispered to Abby. "Did you get the shampoo?"

She nodded. "Teresa dropped if off as promised. I have it with me."

Matt swung open the door, and Austin Briggs, AKA Austin Wells, stepped inside.

He greeted Matt, Abby, and me.

"I don't think I've met these other gentlemen," Austin said as his smile faded.

"This is my fiancé, Jason." Abby said. "He's a landscaper, and he's interested in investing too. This is his business partner." Abby introduced Detective Cooper simply as Bill Cooper.

"We have lots of clients who have pets," Jason said.

Austin's smile reappeared. He saw another sucker.

"Do you have any products that will help with backyard clean-up, such as pooper scoopers?" Bill Cooper asked.

"We do, but you won't make money selling merchandise. As landscapers, however, I'm sure you have plenty of contacts and would be able to sell a substantial number of franchises. That's where the big money is."

I ushered everyone toward the kitchen table and began serving coffee. On the counter, next to the coffee maker, was an unopened bottle of Ajax Shampoo—the one my mom gave me for the dogs. I don't know if Austin noticed it.

I had the company catalog, which my mother had borrowed from Marcia Silver. Matt picked it up and said, "This catalog doesn't have any online address or phone number where a customer can order products."

"That's because you can't order directly," Austin explained. "If a customer wants an item, they need to contact a franchise owner who calls it into me. All franchise owners have my personal cell phone number."

Which I'm sure is a burner and will disappear when you disappear, I thought. I hoped my face didn't show my anger.

"Once again, I want to stress the sale of franchises, not products, is your road to riches." Austin sounded a bit exasperated.

"Can you give me some statistics," Matt asked. "How many franchises, on average, does a franchise owner sell?"

"It varies."

"How about a ballpark figure?" Matt asked again. "Since a franchise will cost me eight thousand dollars, I'd need to sell ten just to recoup my investment."

Austin leaned forward and rested his arms on the table. "I'd say a good salesman could easily sell twenty. That's double your investment. And every time one of your customers sells a franchise to someone else, you get a cut."

He sat back and added, "You could triple your investment. There is no limit."

"Marcia Silver and Fran Foote haven't sold any," I said. "And Marcia's friend Betty sold only one."

"The people sitting with us at last week's dinner sales meeting didn't have any luck either," Abby added. "Gustave sold one and Jack and Jill none."

"I can't help it if some people don't try. There are folks who are not good at selling. But I can tell by talking with you, how skilled you are in the art of persuasion. You will sell. Trust me."

Trust me? I think not. I shook my head.

"We have enough information, Mr. Briggs," Detective Cooper said as he stood up.

Austin's eyes widened and his face appeared on fire,

apparently startled that someone knew his real name. "Who are you?"

"I'm not a landscaper. I'm a police detective. You're under arrest for operating a pyramid scheme which is illegal."

"It's not a pyramid scheme," Austin protested. "We sell products as well as franchises." He pointed to the bottle of dog shampoo on the counter. "You have one of our products right there."

"You have a few products to cover you," I said. "This way the operation doesn't appear as a pyramid. But you actively discourage sales, and many times it's impossible to get the merchandise."

"There's another issue," Jason said. "And probably a lawsuit too. We believe you repackaged the dog shampoo that you bought from Omega Animal Grooming Supplies and are selling under your label at a higher price."

"That's ridiculous." Austin sputtered. His gaze moved from person to person.

"You received a delivery from Omega at your house in Tarrytown. Why would you order products from another pet supply company?" I asked.

"You can't prove any of this." His voice was sparked with anger, but he was shaking like a nervous Chihuahua.

"We're having the two shampoos chemically analyzed tomorrow," Jason said as Abby pulled the bottle of Omega shampoo out of her bag.

"I'm not saying another word until I talk to my attorney."

Detective Cooper left with Austin Briggs in handcuffs.

"I think we can use something stronger than coffee." Matt poured four glasses of wine.

"Archie and Brandy haven't stopped barking from the moment Austin arrived," Abby said. She put the coffee cups in the dishwasher and grabbed a wine glass from her father.

I quickly took a sip of wine. "I'm going to release the dogs from upstairs now. I'll see if Merlin wants to come down too."

As I trudged up the stairs, I breathed a sigh of relief. The pyramid scam was uncovered, although it remained to be seen if there was any money left to return to the victims.

But the murder at the animal sanctuary still remained an unsolved puzzle.

I was meeting Wendy tomorrow. Hopefully, whatever she wanted to show me would break the case wide open.

CHAPTER 44

Sometimes a day starts off bad and spirals downhill.

My coffee machine broke. Matt ran out to get us our caffeine fix but didn't notice when the barrister poured milk into mine—I only drink my coffee black. He brought it home and Archie hit the cup with his wagging tail. The coffee spilled on my new white skirt.

It's always the little things in life that drive you crazy.

After changing my clothes, I was about to leave when I heard a crash. I ran into the living room and found innocent looking Brandy, Archie, and Merlin standing by my favorite vase, now shattered into pieces on the floor.

"Who did this?"

The look from each one said: *Not me. It was the other guy.*

After cleaning the mess, I drove to the animal sanctuary. The facility was taking in a giraffe and a zebra today. These animals had been part of a roadside zoo. I had scheduled an interview first with Gina. She would fill me in on the new arrivals.

Upon entering the administration building, I noticed Wendy was not at the reception desk. I wondered if she was on an errand.

Gina's office door was open, and she motioned me in. The door to Lee's office was also ajar, and I spotted him pecking at his computer keyboard.

"Where's Wendy?" I asked as I slid into a chair across from Gina.

Gina frowned. "I have no idea. She didn't show up today."

"She didn't call?"

Gina sighed and raised her arms. "What can I say? You know college students."

I did, and most are responsible. Wendy struck me as a career oriented young person. I was surprised she wouldn't call if something came up. We had an appointment for later too, and I wondered if she would show for that.

Gina got down to the business at hand. "The giraffe and zebra are old. In addition to increased medical costs, the roadside zoo found that young animals attract more visitors and increase revenue. To them, it's all about the bottom line. The zoo was going to euthanize these two poor guys."

Gina shook her head in disgust. "Happy Place intervened, and the giraffe and zebra will be spending the rest of their lives here."

I asked a few questions and glanced at my watch. "I better go. I'm meeting Nick and Declan at eleven when the animals arrive. I'm observing the giraffe and zebra as they're introduced into their new homes."

Gina frowned. "I'm sorry. I guess no one told you."

"Told me what?"

"There's been a delay. The animals won't arrive until four this afternoon. Can you be here then?"

I groaned. My day wasn't getting better.

"Yes," I said, although somewhat wearily. "I can be here."

I was about to ask another question when Lee stepped into the room.

"Ready, Gina?" he asked.

Gina nodded and said to me, "Lee and I have a luncheon in Manhattan. The luncheon sponsor is an association of non-profit organizations, and the guest speaker's topic is *Raising Money and Spending It Wisely.*"

I wanted to question Gina about how she felt when she discovered Maureen's role in her father's disbarment. Unfortunately, it appeared I'd lost my window of opportunity. She rose to leave. My questions would have to wait.

We all departed the building. Lee and Gina headed toward the parking lot while I stood for a moment, pondering my next course of action.

My appointment with Wendy, if she showed, was in a little more than two hours. I had no desire to drive back home or to my office for that short time. I found a bench under a large oak overlooking the wolves. I decided to write my story on the pyramid scam. I had all my notes with me.

The tree shade combined with the light summer breeze made this a delightful place to work. I pulled my laptop out of my bag and began. A few minutes before one o'clock, I put my writing away. I'd finished the story.

I made my way to the fox habitat where Wendy and I planned to rendezvous. She wasn't there. I waited for thirty minutes. She didn't show.

I silently reprimanded myself for not getting her cell number.

I glanced at my watch. The giraffe and zebra wouldn't arrive for two and a half hours, so I had time to kill. I left the sanctuary and drove to the nearest shopping mall where I purchased a new coffee maker. After that, I stopped at a café in a local strip mall for a late lunch. I still had time before the animals arrived, but I decided to make my way back to the sanctuary. Perhaps Wendy was there now or had called the office to explain her absence.

I stepped out of the cafe and was about to hop into my car when I noticed a construction site across the road. A large sign read:

New Condominium Development
Opening Soon
Garone Construction

Garone construction was the company owned by Gina's husband. I decided to satisfy my curiosity and take a look.

I left my car in the café parking lot and crossed the road. No one was working at the site which was odd for mid-afternoon of a weekday. It looked as if no one had been working for quite a while.

I spotted an architectural rendition next to the sign. The drawing featured a planned community with one-story garden apartment units spread across a large expanse of land.

I peered through the wire fence that had been set up around the perimeter along with NO TRESPASSING signs about every six feet. It appeared that construction had barely begun.

I crossed back to the café and decided to get a coffee *to go*. I didn't need more caffeine, but I wanted to question the staff about the construction site. Maybe someone knew something.

"That condo project doesn't look as if it will be opening soon," I said to the counter server as she poured my coffee. She was slight of build with gray hair in a bun.

She shrugged but didn't respond. "Milk? Sugar?"

"Plain black coffee. It looks like the crew stopped working?"

"They have."

"How long ago did they stop?"

"Not sure. Couple weeks, maybe."

"Do you know why?"

"Why? What do you mean?"

Getting information from this woman was like getting a bone away from a dog. "Why they stopped?"

"Haven't a clue."

This was a dead end. I paid for my coffee and left.

As I headed for my car, I noticed a bar located at the end of this strip mall. Bartenders sometimes can be talkative.

"What the heck, I'll give it a try," I mumbled. I stashed my coffee in my car and made my way to the Tortoise and Hare Bar.

The door was slightly ajar, so I peeked before entering. Two middle-aged women were sitting at a table in the back. A large, ruddy faced man with a bulbous nose was perched on a bar stool near the front.

I stepped inside onto a sticky floor. The scent of stale beer wafted through the room. It took a moment for my eyes to adjust to the darkness.

I approached the bar and positioned myself about two stools down from the man with the bulbous nose. He nodded to me. A half empty glass of what appeared to be beer was in front of him. Judging from the glazed look in his eyes, it wasn't his first drink of the day.

The bartender was a woman. Her skin was wrinkled and dry, which I suspected came from long hours in the sun. I couldn't tell her age, but I guessed she looked older than she was.

"What can I get you?" she asked.

"Coca-Cola. What's going on at the construction company across the street?" I asked. "Looks like they stopped work."

"They did. Three weeks ago. They were here on a Friday and never came back on Monday."

"I wonder why?"

The bartender shook her head. "There are rumors, but I don't know if they're true."

"Sometimes rumors hold the truth." I would never include an unsubstantiated rumor in one of my stories, but I would investigate.

"I heard the builder ran out of money," she said as she handed me my soda.

The man with the beer nodded his head. "Yup. Probably

true." He took a swig of his drink.

The bartender spoke up again. "I miss them. They were good for business, and most of the workers were great tippers."

As I sipped my soda, I wondered if lack of money was why the work had stopped. But there were dozens of other reasons to halt construction—municipal permit problems, starting or completing other projects, and delays in obtaining supplies were just a few.

Whatever the reason, I concluded it couldn't have any bearing on Maureen McDermott's murder.

At least, I didn't think so.

I was worried about Wendy.

I arrived back at the sanctuary a few minutes before four o'clock. As I pulled into a parking space, another car sped into the lot and parked in a spot directly across from me—one that was designated for staff parking. Lee emerged from the driver's side, and Gina hoped out of the front passenger seat.

"How was the luncheon?" I asked as I caught up with them.

"Good." As we all headed toward the administration building, Gina told me about it.

"I left my phone in my car," Lee said to Gina once we almost reached our destination. "I need to go back and get it. I'll catch up with you in the office."

Lee turned and headed back to the parking lot.

This would give me the opportunity to talk privately with Gina.

"Have you heard from Wendy?" I asked.

Gina shook her head. "No. And despite what I said earlier about unreliable college kids, this really is unlike Wendy. I hope she's OK."

I did too. I then dropped my bombshell question. I asked

Gina about her father's disbarment and the role Maureen played.

"You know about my father's disbarment?" she asked. Her eyes widened in alarm. "Are you writing about it in your story?"

"As long as it has nothing to do with the sanctuary, it will remain our secret."

"She sighed. "Thank you. I don't want it rehashed. I promise you, it has nothing to do with the sanctuary. I only found out about Maureen's involvement at my dad's funeral."

"That's why your attitude toward her changed?"

Gina nodded. "Once I discovered who she was, I hated her. But I had nothing to do with her murder."

Gina and I parted. She entered the administration building, and I took off to meet Declan and Nick.

The giraffe and zebra arrived shortly. Declan gave them a brief exam, and they were released into their new habitat.

I love all animals, but there is something about the soul of an older animal that is shown in its eyes.

Declan left, but Nick and I remained. We were watching the giraffe and zebra adjust to their surroundings when Nick's phone trilled.

His face paled as he listened to his caller.

"I'll go over there right now." He ended the conversation.

"What's wrong?" I asked.

"That was Gina. The police are here. They received an anonymous call. There's a dead body in the sanctuary."

CHAPTER 45

I tasted bile. I had a premonition of who it was.

Gina told Nick the body was by the pond at the north end of the property. We hopped into one of the sanctuary's pick-up trucks and drove on the bumpy road north to our destination. The area was cordoned off with yellow crime scene tape and was swarming with law enforcement. Two police cars and a crime scene van sat in the dirt parking lot.

I spotted Gina Garone.

"Do you know who it is yet?" Nick asked Gina as we jumped out of the truck.

She nodded. I sucked in my breath.

"It's Wendy."

That had been my premonition. "How did she die?"

"I don't know. Apparently, there was no sign of struggle."

"Why would anyone want to kill her?" Nick asked. "Everyone liked Wendy."

Rather than answering with the obvious, "not everyone," I said, "It may be connected to Maureen's murder."

"How?" Nick and Gina asked at the same time.

I shrugged. "I have no idea. But two murders here during a two-week period…"

I didn't finish my statement. I was writing a story on the sanctuary, and Wendy wanted to meet with me. It couldn't be a coincidence. I didn't know if I could trust Nick or Gina.

Before I could say anything else, a Crown Victoria careened into the parking lot. No doubt Detective Wolfe was inside.

I was right. Wolfe emerged from the car. His normally blank expression turned into a scowl once he spotted me. Detective Fox, who was with him, grinned slightly.

"Once again, you are at a crime scene," Wolfe said through gritted teeth.

"Nick and I arrived only a minute ago. We'd heard about the body."

"Were you here before the police?" Wolfe asked. He continued glaring at me.

"No." I shook my head.

"Then you are not a witness and shouldn't be loitering. Do not, I repeat, do not go anywhere near the crime scene tape, and do not bother the investigators."

Nick, Gina, and I moved back as Wolfe lifted the yellow tape and made his way toward the body. Fox followed.

"We might as well leave," Nick said.

"I'm staying," Gina replied. "The press will be calling, so the more I know the better I can answer their questions."

"I'll stay too," I said.

"Okay." Nick nodded. "I'm going. If anyone wants me, I'll be with the giraffe and zebra." He hopped in his truck and drove away.

The medical examiner's van pulled into the lot, and their staff entered the crime scene. Gina and I waited, but the body was too far back to see anything. After a while, the medical examiner's staff removed the corpse.

Wolfe and Fox were the last to emerge. I think Wolfe wore the same brown suit every time I saw him.

"How did she die?" I asked.

"You need to wait for the autopsy," Wolfe snapped back.

Fox winked at me. I would call him later.

Once the two detectives departed, Gina shook her head. "These murders could do major damage to our fundraising efforts."

I frowned. "Plus, Wendy and Maureen lost their lives."

"I didn't mean it the way it sounded, but we do good work at the sanctuary. I'd hate to see it close because we can't raise the money needed to keep us going." She paused. "C'mon. I'll give you a ride back."

We drove away in silence. Two people were dead. A killer was on the loose. And Gina was right. The sanctuary saved countless animals, and it survived on donations. This could destroy it. These murders needed to be solved, and this needed to be done quickly.

Later that evening, I phoned Detective Fox on this cell.

"Do you have any idea of cause of death?" I asked.

"Not yet. There was nothing obvious like a gunshot or stab wound. The medical examiner will check for poisons, especially etorphine."

"Do you know time of death yet?"

"There is a general idea based on the level of rigor mortis. It was determined she probably died between noon and three in the afternoon. The autopsy may narrow it down more."

My stomach flip-flopped. I believed Wendy's and Maureen's murders were connected. There were five suspects in Maureen's murder: Gina, Lee, Nick, Sam, and Declan.

Gina and Lee had been in their offices today when I arrived at ten-thirty, and they left together for their luncheon in Manhattan at eleven. Their attendance at the luncheon would be easy to verify. They returned to the sanctuary together at four. I saw them.

They had alibis between noon and three.
That narrowed the suspect list to Nick, Sam, and Declan.

CHAPTER 46

"None of the motives work," I said later that evening.

"Why not?" Abby asked. She rubbed the back of her neck.

I had created a suspect board and placed it on an easel adjacent to my kitchen table. Abby had come to the house to help me make sense of the information we had.

"In most cases, we've been looking at revenge against Maureen as a motive for her murder," I said. "Vengeance for her past action."

"Except for Declan. His motive is different," Abby added, "The charge of misconduct brought against him by Maureen—that charge goes away now that she's dead."

"But why kill Wendy?" I sipped my wine. "None of these motives have anything to do with her."

"Maybe Wendy knew who murdered Maureen, and the killer needed to keep her quiet," Abby suggested.

"Wendy was on vacation at the time of Maureen's death—she was out of the state." I shook my head. "We're looking at this from the wrong angle."

"What do you mean?"

"I now believe the murders of Maureen and Wendy involve a wrongdoing at the sanctuary."

"A wrongdoing? Like what?"

"I don't know." I shrugged. "But Wendy was the receptionist. She handled phone calls and the mail. She entered data into the computer. She knew everything that happened."

I stroked Merlin, who had curled up on my lap. "Don't forget. She wanted to show me something the day she was murdered. Something is going on in the sanctuary, and I'm sure Wendy knew or suspected it."

"But how can this tie into Maureen? She didn't work in the office. She was an animal keeper. Did she have privy to information?"

"Maureen possessed an attorney's eye. Her training would cause her to read everything and investigate whatever seemed out of place." I paused. "Is something wrong with your neck?" I noticed my daughter touching it a second time.

"I was jogging in the park before I came here, and I think I was stung by a wasp or some sort of insect."

"Do you want me to look—?"

"I'm fine. If it acts up, I've medication at home. Let's get back to the case."

"If we can find out what was happening at the sanctuary, it could lead us to the killer." I said.

An image popped into my mind. I phoned Detective Fox on his cell. When he picked up, I told him Abby was here, and the phone was on speaker. Then, I got right to the point.

"Did Wendy have a purse or carryall when her body was found?" I asked.

"No. Why do you ask?"

"Because it is strange for a woman not to have a bag with her."

"The body may have been moved."

"What about her phone? Did she have it on her?"

"No. All we found was the body. She was wearing pants. They had two pockets, but both were empty."

"Gina said the police received an anonymous phone call about the body. Do you know if the caller was male or female?" I asked.

"I never heard the voice but was told the tape was doctored, so we can't be sure."

"You've no idea who reported it?"

"Absolutely none." He paused. "We couldn't trace it. The call came from a burner."

I digested what I knew. Eventually the body would have been discovered. Whoever called wanted it found at a specific time.

I wondered why?

"One final question for now," I said. "Do you have any clues at all as to who murdered Wendy?"

"Not yet. I just got home from her apartment where a search was conducted. Nothing relating to her murder was found. Both her home and work computers have been impounded. The tech staff will check them tomorrow."

"What about her desk at work?"

"We went through that too and found nothing of interest. But as I said, we took the computer."

"Is that all you took?"

"Yes. That's what Wolfe thought was important."

I had a lot of things to think about but nothing more to ask at the present time, so I said good-bye.

"I know that look," Abby said as I placed my phone back on the table. "You're hatching a plan."

I held up two fingers. "Twice, I spotted Wendy frowning at something in a notebook. Both times, she stashed that notebook in the top side drawer of her desk." Brandy, who was curled up next to me, pricked her ears. I swear she liked to listen to my conversations and knew when I was about to say something interesting.

"But Detective Fox told us the police found nothing." Abby

said.

"Maybe it's because they don't know what to look for."

"Do you?"

"I'm not sure. But I plan to find out."

Abby folded her arms in front. "And how to you plan to do this?"

"My first step is to question the suspects about the daily operations of the sanctuary, especially any schedules they follow. I want to see if one of them tells a different story than the others. That might provide a place to start."

"You said that's your first step. What's next?"

"Wendy's notebook is probably still in her desk, because Wolfe didn't think it was important. I need to get hold of it."

CHAPTER 47

The morning rush hour traffic would give Mother Teresa road rage. Still, I left the house with time to spare and arrived early at the sanctuary. I figured Nick would still be at the food storage building loading up his supplies for the day.

"The road to the storage area is unpaved," the guard at the entrance booth reminded me. "So you need to drive slowly. You don't want to break an axle."

I agreed.

Instead of heading into the main parking lot, I veered left and traveled the bumpy road to the storage facilities. When I arrived Nick was outside, loading crates of food onto his truck.

"I figured you would be back," Nick called once he spotted me. "I heard the suspects have been narrowed down to the three who were at the sanctuary during the time of Wendy's murder. That includes me."

I nodded. "Can you account for your time between noon and three yesterday?" I went straight to the point.

"I was in my office at the other end of the sanctuary going over inventory figures. But no one was with me to verify this."

"Do you know where Sam and Declan were?"

"Sam was repainting the small barn. If you look, you'll see a fresh coat of paint that wasn't there the day before." He paused. "But I don't know how long the painting took."

"You're saying he could have finished his painting early and still had time to commit the murder, or he might have killed Wendy first and then painted the barn?"

Nick nodded. "It's possible. In the early morning, we all have set chores and can usually be found at specific locations. But for the rest of the day, staff could be anywhere."

"Do you know where Declan was at the time of Wendy's murder?"

Nick shook his head. "He often does a drive and stop in the afternoon, but I can't be sure."

"What's a drive and stop?"

"That's what we call it when he rides around the facility in his pick-up truck and stops at the various habitats to observe the animals. This is one way he checks to make sure nothing is wrong. Behavior can tell a lot about an animal's health."

Before I could speak, Nick added, "During a drive and stop, he could be at any location. We have several dozen habitats."

I sighed. "So once again, as in the case with Maureen McDermott, no one has a verifiable alibi."

"Although no one has a solid alibi for either Maureen or Wendy's death, there's a big difference with the two murders," Nick replied. "Walk with me, and we can finish talking while I get more food for wolves and bobcat."

I followed him into the building and into the refrigerated section. I shivered. Nick continued, "Unlike Maureen, no one hated Wendy. I know I said this before, but I believe it's key to this case."

I didn't know that much about Wendy. I needed to perform due diligence and check her out. But for the most part, I agreed with Nick. Wendy's death wasn't personal.

That's why I was sure Wendy's murder had something to do with the sanctuary. I believed it was related to illegal activity that she and Maureen had both discovered.

Nick lifted up a box marked *Wolves.* I assumed it was their food. As I glanced on the floor, I spotted something shiny.

"What's this?" I asked as I bent down to pick it up.

It was a gold necklace with the letter *W* hanging from the chain.

"This is Wendy's necklace," I said, answering my own question. "She wore it the last time I saw her."

CHAPTER 48

"**B**ut Wendy never came to the storage units." Nick scratched his head. "How did her necklace get here?"

This storage unit was probably less than a quarter of a mile from the pond where Wendy's body was found. Was she murdered here and dragged to the pond area? If so, what was she doing inside the storage unit?

I was sure Wendy's notebook held the key to her murder. I had to find a way to get into her desk.

"I'll give the necklace to Detective Fox," I said as I stuffed it in my pocket. "It could be a clue." I had no more questions for Nick, so I said good-bye, hopped into my car, and drove back to the administration building. After parking my car, I scurried up the path to my destination.

I was almost there when I heard angry whispers echoing against the trees. I spotted two women next to the heavily wooded area on the side of the building. It was Gina Garone and Carolyn Whitcome. Gina was gesturing with her hands.

After circling around and stepping into the wooded area. I crept quietly until reaching a spot where I wouldn't be seen, but where I could hear their conversation.

"Why are the costs so high?" Carolyn asked. "They've skyrocketed since the sanctuary opened."

"We've taken in several large animals, and their food costs

are enormous," Gina answered. "We've also been acquiring older animals, and that means increased medical expenses."

"If we can't cut costs, we need to raise more money."

"With these two murders, fundraising won't be easy."

"Think of something. That's your job. Otherwise we'll be forced to close."

"No. That can't happen." I could hear the distress in Gina's voice. "We've worked too hard."

"At the very least, we'll need to transfer some of the high maintenance animals to facilities in other parts of the country. We should sit down with Lee and work out a plan."

"Please. Not yet. Lee cares about the numbers, not the animals. Give me a little more time. I'll see what I can do."

Silence. Carolyn finally spoke. "I'll give you two weeks but no longer."

I watched Gina and Carolyn depart. Carolyn took off toward the parking lot while Gina made her way into the administration building.

I waved my hand to shoo away a large mosquito, and I was heading out of the woods when Declan wandered up the path.

"Declan," I called.

He stopped. His face was despondent.

"Detective Wolfe grilled me for nearly an hour," he said. "He told me not to leave town. He thinks I killed both Wendy and Maureen."

Declan ran his fingers through his hair. "He said he'll have me in cuffs if it's the last thing he does."

"Where were you when Wendy's murder took place?" I asked.

"Doing a drive and stop. After that I was treating a monkey with an ingrown toenail." Before I could react, he added, "But no one saw me."

A dozen thoughts squirreled through my mind, but one kept popping up. "I need to get into Wendy's desk. Is it locked?"

Declan shook his head. "I don't think so. The police went through it, but they didn't find anything."

"That's because they don't know what they are looking for." I frowned. "Wolfe thinks you're the murderer. He's only searching for evidence to support his theory. If he didn't think there was anything in the desk to incriminate you, he wouldn't check any further."

We both stood silently for a moment before I made a decision.

I didn't believe Declan was the killer. But if I was to prove his innocence, I'd need his help.

"Gina went into the building a few minutes ago," I told him. "Do you think Lee is also there?"

Declan shook his head. "I heard he's at a meeting in the city and won't be back until later."

"Would anyone else be in the building?"

Declan shrugged. "I doubt it. Probably just Gina."

"I'd like you to go into Gina's office and keep her occupied for a few moments. You'll also need to make sure her office door is shut, so she can't see the reception desk."

He narrowed his eyes and folded his arms in front of his chest. "Why?"

"I need to rummage through Wendy's desk. I'm looking—"

"You can't do that." He was shaking his head before I finished talking. "And I can't help you. I'm in enough trouble."

"If we don't find the real murderer, you'll be in a lot more trouble."

"What do you mean?"

"*You'll* be arrested for murder."

CHAPTER 49

"This could be a disaster," Declan said, grumbling. "But okay. I'll do it."

"Good." I smiled. "I'll need time to search. How will you stall?"

"Stall?" He looked like a deer caught in the headlights, but in a few seconds, he grinned. "I'll tell Gina about my idea to raise funds. She should produce a calendar with each month featuring a photo of a different animal from the sanctuary. She could sell the calendars online. I know of a few animal rescue organizations doing this."

I nodded. I was aware of this too. "But you need to talk about this idea long enough to give me time."

"I'll try," he added after a moment of hesitation.

He appeared a bit unsure, which did not inspire confidence. But this was the only plan I had to find the notebook.

"Take out your phone now and text me '*go*' but don't send it yet," I said. "As soon as you're in Gina's office with the door shut, press *send*. Once I receive it, I'll enter the building and rummage through Wendy's desk."

"Okay." He pulled out his phone and scrolled down.

"When I find the notebook, I'll text you the letter '*G*' for *Go*. You can wrap up your conversation and leave."

As Declan swung open the door and was about to enter the

administration building, I reminded him, "Don't forget to shut her office door, so she doesn't see me."

"That might not be easy. Gina usually keeps her door open when meeting with someone, especially staff. If I push too hard, she'll get suspicious."

Declan entered the building. I pulled out my phone, nervously waiting to hear from him. Finally, he sent the text. I stepped inside and immediately noticed that the door to Gina's office was partially ajar. But Declan stood in front of her desk. He was a towering figure, so I felt pretty sure he blocked her view of the reception area—at least I hoped he did.

I approached Wendy's desk and pulled open the drawer where she had last stashed the notebook.

IT WASN'T THERE.

Did the police take it? But Detective Fox told me they found nothing of interest. All they removed was the computer.

Where was the notebook?

I checked the other three drawers. All I found was stationary and two chocolate bars.

I was so intent on searching I didn't hear the front door creak open.

But I heard the voice.

"What are you doing?" he bellowed.

I jerked my head up and experienced that sinking feeling in the pit of my stomach.

The voice belonged to Detective Wolfe.

CHAPTER 50

"I asked you what you are doing."

"Looking for a pencil." It was the first thought that came to mind.

"This is a crime scene."

"No. It's not. I don't see the crime scene tape," I said, defiantly. "And I see the computer is missing, so you must have taken it."

Wolfe narrowed his eyes to tiny slits. "I don't believe for one second that you're searching for a pencil. You're snooping. You're interfering with a criminal investigation. I could—"

"What's going on," Gina called. She and Declan emerged from her office. Declan mouthed the word "sorry," so I assumed he couldn't stall her any longer. I hoped Wolfe wouldn't mention that he caught me searching through Wendy's desk.

Luckily, he didn't have time to say anything. Gina spotted him and said, "Can I help you Detective Wolfe?"

"I need to talk with you—privately." He emphasized the last word. "Let's go into your office."

Before going further, he waved a fat finger in Declan's face. "You wait out here. I'll have more questions for you after I finish with the director."

Declan and I exchanged worried glances.

Detective Wolfe stomped off into Gina's office. Before Gina joined him, she turned toward my direction. She looked surprised to see me but not happy.

"What brings you here today?" she asked.

Thinking as fast as I could, I said, "I was wondering if any funeral arrangements have been made for Wendy."

"The autopsy needs to be completed before the body is released. Meanwhile, her parents live in California and will be flying here. I don't know if they made any funeral plans yet. They haven't contacted me. They've been dealing with her roommate."

"Do you have a phone number for Wendy's roommate?"

Gina narrowed her eyes. "Why? You hardly know Wendy."

"Not true. I did get to know her. We talked about her dream of becoming a veterinarian. I also lent her one of my husband's veterinary books, and I'd like to get it back."

That seemed to satisfy Gina. She nodded and pulled out her phone. While scrolling down, she said, "Wendy's roommate's name is Sharika. She phoned me this morning, so let me check my recent calls."

"I'm waiting," Wolfe yelled. He was seated in Gina's office.

"I'll be right there." Gina scrolled down and gave me Sharika's number.

I had more questions for Gina, but I wasn't asking them with Wolfe around. I said good-bye and left the building. Declan remained inside, waiting as the detective had told him to do.

While making my way to the parking lot, I phoned Sharika.

"This is Kristy Farrell," I said when she answered. "I knew your roommate Wendy and I wanted to—"

"I'm so glad you called," Sharika interrupted. "I need to speak with you."

"You do? I didn't think you knew who I was."

"Wendy talked about you. The night before she was killed, she said if anything happened to her, I should contact you."

CHAPTER 51

Sharika was in-between classes and had time to see me now. She and Wendy had shared a student apartment, off campus.

During my drive to Sharika's place, I stopped at police headquarters to give Wendy's necklace to Detective Fox.

"This could be a clue," I said.

"Maybe," he shrugged. "I better go and log this in. Thanks for bringing it to me. Johnson, will you escort Mrs. Farrell out?"

I wanted to ask him why he hadn't accompanied Wolfe to the sanctuary today, but he didn't seem anxious to have a conversation.

I left police headquarters. When I arrived at Sharika's apartment, she buzzed me in. Since there was no elevator, I trudged up the two flights of stairs to the third floor. Sharika, who was waiting by the door of her unit, had a model's figure— tall and sleek. Her skin was the color of coffee au lait.

As I stepped inside, two cats, one calico and the other gray, scurried off to another room.

"Those were Wendy's kitties," Sharika said. "I guess they're mine now."

Sharika led me into her tiny living room.

"I'm glad you called," she said, once we were seated. "Wendy told me to talk to you, but she never left a phone number. She told me you worked for *Animal Advocate Magazine*, so I planned to reach you there."

"Did Wendy say why you should contact me?"

Sadness appeared in Sharika's dark brown eyes as she nodded and answered. "Wendy thought her life was in danger. At the time, I thought she was overly melodramatic, but I was wrong—really wrong.

"Why did Wendy think she was in danger?"

Sharika hesitated. "She uncovered a problem at the animal sanctuary, but she never told me what it was."

Dozens of thoughts flashed through my mind as I wondered what the problem could be. Animal abuse... using animals for canned hunts... health violations... misuse of funds... selling drugs... the list could go on. Maybe someone discovered contamination of the underground water supply. Perhaps the animals were conduits for smuggling contraband. I had a vivid imagination.

"Wendy claimed what she discovered was illegal," Sharika said. "She confronted someone at the sanctuary who denied his involvement but said he knew about the crimes and was trying to gather evidence. He arranged to meet Wendy the next day and explain everything. She—"

"Who was this person?" I interrupted.

"I've no idea," Sharika said, "but I do know it was a man. She always used the pronoun *he*. Anyway, he told Wendy not to mention their upcoming meeting with anyone.

"But she told you?"

Sharika nodded. "She finally admitted to the meeting, but refused to identify the man. She thought this man could be guilty but wanted to hear his side of the story. Wendy didn't like gossip and rumors. I knew I wouldn't get more out of her until she was sure of all her facts."

Sharika emitted a small sob. "But she was afraid. I told her not to go. I told her to call the police and let them handle it.

But to tell the truth, I didn't push, because I thought she was exaggerating. And she claimed they were meeting in a public place. I was pretty sure she said a diner."

"Did she say what diner?"

Sharika shook her head. "No. But she was worried about making it to work on time. She said as long as the meeting wasn't longer than thirty minutes, she'd be okay."

I let this sink in. Wendy was planning on going to work. Her job started at eight.

"What time did she leave here?"

"About six-forty five."

I did some quick calculations in my head. That meant she had to drive to the diner, have a half hour meeting, and arrive at the sanctuary, all in one hour and fifteen minutes. How many diners were close enough for her to do this?

I spotted a photograph of Wendy and Sharika on an end table. It was a picture of them at the beach.

"May I borrow this photo?" I asked.

"Sure. But why?"

"I'm going to visit all the diners within a specific radius of the animal sanctuary and show them this picture. Maybe one of the staff will recognize Wendy. If so, that person may also be able to identify her table companion, who is most likely her killer."

"Isn't that like searching for a needle in a haystack?" Sharika asked.

I grinned. "Yes, but more like a large knitting needle. It will be difficult but not impossible."

I realized, however, that during the breakfast rush, Long Island diners were busy. It could be no one would remember Wendy.

I sat back and sighed. "I wish we had more clues."

"Maybe there are clues in her notebook," Sharika said.

"Notebook!" I almost jumped out of my chair.

"If something happened to Wendy, she said I was to give it to you."

"What about the police?"

"Before the police came, I stashed it in my dresser. I know Wendy wanted you to have it. She was afraid to keep it at the sanctuary anymore, so when she met with you, she was planning on bringing you back here. I'll get it now."

When Sharika returned from the bedroom, she said, "Unfortunately, Wendy used lots of abbreviations. Whenever she wrote reminders, she only used the first letter of a word. It drove me crazy."

"Is that what she did in her notebook?"

Sharika nodded. "The night before her murder she told me she was going to explain it all when she met up with you. But now you'll need to figure this out yourself."

Sharika handed the notebook to me, and added, "I looked at what she wrote. I haven't a clue what anything means. Hopefully, you can decipher it."

I thumbed through the pages. Most were blank. She'd only written on the first two.

On page one was a chart with a series of letters and numbers. Page two had letters and question marks.

I'd no idea what anything meant.

CHAPTER 52

"This makes no sense." I sat by my kitchen table where I was trying, unsuccessfully, to decipher the following chart in Wendy's notebook.

	D	P	N	
M	10,000p	10,000 p	15,000 p	(5,000)
F	15,000 p	40,000p	45,000 p	(10,000)

I moved on to the second page which simply listed five letters, with each one followed by a question mark.

P?
B?
G?
A?
B?

"I've no idea what words these letters represent?" I said to Abby, who sat next to me sipping wine. I pointed to the vertical line of letters—M and F, and then to the next page with P, B, G, A, and B. I loved puzzles, but I hadn't a clue as to how to solve this one.

My daughter scrutinized the two pages. "Could each be the first letter of one of the sanctuary animals?"

I studied the list as I scratched behind Merlin's ear. The cat was curled up on my lap.

"M for monkey, F for fox," I mumbled and then turned the page. "P could be for pelican, B could be bear, and G might represent giraffe. But I don't remember any animal at the sanctuary that begins with A."

"No aardvarks or apes?"

"None. Nor antelope or alpaca. I have a list of all the animals at the sanctuary," I said. "I stuffed it in my bag on the first day I visited. Let me get it. We can check if I'm missing something."

My tote rested on the kitchen counter. I gently lifted Merlin and placed him on Abby's lap, so I could get up and fetch the list. Cats don't take kindly to humans moving them. He jumped to the floor and bolted out of the room.

I made my way to the counter, and after rummaging through my belongings, I pulled out the list. I was right. Nothing began with A.

Abby and I sat silently. I thought back to one of the first stories I wrote for *Animal Advocate*. I'd interviewed a special agent for the United States Fish and Wildlife Service. He'd told me how animals were used to smuggle contraband.

"Maybe these letters stand for drugs that are being transported inside the animals."

Abby tilted her head. "It's possible. These letters could stand for anything. But what about the letters running across the top of the first page—D, P, and N?"

Abby pulled out her phone and snapped a picture of the pages. "I'll show these to Declan. Maybe he'll recognize something."

"I should text these pages to Detective Fox, too." I said. "I need to keep him in the loop."

As I grabbed my phone, I remembered he hadn't returned

my earlier call, which was unlike him. I texted a photo of the pages and reminded him we needed to talk.

"Do you think he'll have an idea what the letters and numbers mean?" Abby asked.

"I doubt it, but it's worth a try."

"Let's get some cheese and crackers," Abby suggested. "My best ideas come to me when I'm eating."

"Me too." I maneuvered around my table to the cabinet for the crackers. Abby grabbed cheese from the refrigerator.

We continued discussing the notebook. But after our snack, we still didn't have any idea as to what the letters and numbers that Wendy had written meant.

"Sometimes the best thing to do is sleep on it." I said, trying not to sound discouraged. "I'll look over the notebook before I go to bed, and maybe when I get up in the morning, something will have popped in my mind."

. Meanwhile, let's hope we have more luck with the diners."

I shut Wendy's notebook and grabbed my laptop. "We need to come up with a list of all diners where Abby might have met with someone. I have a list of the communities where she could have been during the time frame that would allow her to get to work by eight."

Abby and I began researching. An hour later, we had our list. But Fox still hadn't contacted me.

"What are you going to do next?" Abby asked.

"I intend to visit each of these diners. I have a photo of Wendy. I'll ask the serving staff if anyone recognizes her."

"What will you do if someone does?"

I grinned. "Monday, I'm heading back to the sanctuary and taking photos of the suspects—Nick, Sam, and…" I hesitated. "Declan." Although I felt in my heart it wasn't Declan, he was one of only three people without an alibi. I had to do due diligence.

"The next day, I'll bring these employee photos with me to the diners," I continued. "If any member of a diner's serving staff recognizes Wendy, I'll see if that person also recognizes any of the three suspects."

"If you want company I can go with you. I'm working evening hours with Dad next week, so I have the mornings off. And I can save you some effort. I have a photo of Declan from the veterinary dinner in Manhattan. Other people are in it, but it's a good shot of him."

"I'll take it. And a picture of Nick and Sam should be easy to get. No one should be suspicious because I'll tell them I need photos to accompany my magazine story."

Merlin came back in and hopped on my lap at the same time my phone trilled. The name Adrian Fox appeared across the screen.

"We have a problem," he said before I had a chance to say more than hello. "Wolfe ordered me to not do any investigating on this case unless he personally okays it. He knows you're involved, and he knows I've been helping you."

"How did he find out?"

"He may not be the brightest bulb, but even he recognizes the obvious. You were there when Wendy's body was discovered. You always seem to turn up at our crime scenes."

My mind wandered back to when Wolfe appeared alone at the sanctuary this morning. Detective Fox was being shut out of the case.

"He told me he spotted you rifling through Wendy's desk today," Fox added, interrupting my thoughts.

"I was, but I've been careful in all I do to make sure he doesn't know I've involved you. There's no connection between us."

Fox sighed. "This may be my fault. Yesterday, I left my phone on my desk when I went to get a soda from the vending machine. I think he scrolled down my recent calls. Your name is there—

numerous times."

"Can he do that? Isn't that illegal?" I had done this with Sam Garcia's phone, but I wasn't a member of law enforcement.

"He'll never admit to searching my phone. But when I returned to the room, it was obvious he knew we'd been talking."

"What did he say?"

"He told me a source told him you were sticking your nose where it didn't belong, and I was aiding and abetting you."

"Aiding and abetting? He actually used those terms? And what's his source? Your phone?"

"I'm pretty sure it is. Anyway, he told me I was not to do anymore investigating into the sanctuary murders unless he gave me a specific assignment. He made a point of saying that included talking to the nosy reporter." Fox paused. "That's you."

"So I surmised," I said, drily.

"Wolfe said this was a direct order. If he caught me disobeying, he would put me on report."

"Why is he so concerned about this investigation?" I asked.

"This is a big case. He wants to arrest Declan Carr. He feels the evidence, although circumstantial, is strong enough for a conviction, and he wants the credit. If he's the one who solves the case, he's positive it will help him cinch a promotion to the next level."

Much of the evidence did weigh heavily toward our veterinarian friend. And Wolfe always looked for the easiest collar.

Juries have been known to convict on circumstantial evidence. I was worried about Declan.

I also was concerned for Detective Fox. Wolfe's uncle was the Deputy Commissioner. If Wolfe put in a complaint, it could ruin my detective's friend's career.

Fox must have sensed what I was thinking. He said, "I have no intention of dropping this case. I don't know if Declan Carr is innocent, but there are too many unanswered questions. I'll continue to investigate and help you, but I have to be careful. If it gets back to him, I'm in trouble."

"Of course."

"Unfortunately, my help will come at a lot slower pace. I can only do it during my time off. Uh oh, I hear Wolfe in the hallway. He's back from the deli. In a few minutes, the entire squad room will smell of garlic. I better end this call."

With that, he was gone.

"What was that about?" Abby asked.

As I related my phone conversation, Merlin jumped off my lap and scooted out of the kitchen as Archie entered. The two animals appeared to get along without any problems, but I'd noticed Merlin preferred to be in a different room than the big dog. Archie was affectionate and loved everyone, including cats, but he could play rough.

Suddenly Archie scurried to the door as I heard the sound of a car pulling into the driveway. Brandy joined him.

"That must be my mother back early."

Abby's eyes widened. "That's not good. She'll want to talk about the wedding, and I'm not ready."

"Maybe she'll want to go straight to bed."

Abby shook her head. "No. She texted me earlier. She said she had another great idea."

CHAPTER 53

Things aren't always as they seem.

"This is why you can never assume," I said to Abby on the phone Monday morning as I drove to the Happy Place Animal Sanctuary. "That includes thoughts expressed by my mother."

My mother's "*great idea*" on Friday night was to hire Marcia Silver's grand-niece to bake the wedding cake. When Abby rolled her eyes at this suggestion, my mother sat back, grinned, and calmly told us the name of Marcia's grand-niece. She then said we needed to check her out. Abby didn't want to have anything to do with this, but last night, she finally decided to conduct an internet search.

"Who would have thought that Marcia was related to one of the leading bakers on Long Island," Abby said. "Her bakery is famous."

"And Marcia said her niece would give you the friends and family discount."

"Maybe I should listen to some of grandma's suggestions. But I'm still not color coordinating the bridesmaids' dresses with the food."

I laughed. "Gotta go now. I'm pulling into the sanctuary."

After parking the car, I made my way up the path to the administration building. Upon entering, I spotted Gina slouched behind her desk, appearing deep in thought. I couldn't be sure, but it sounded as if she groaned when she spotted me.

But she motioned me into her office.

"I need photos of Nick and Sam. I hoped you might have a general idea where they are this morning." I grinned. "That way I won't be wandering aimlessly around this place."

She glanced at her watch. "At this time, Sam's probably with either the donkeys or the llamas. That should at least narrow it down."

She brushed away a wisp of hair that had fallen in front of her eyes, and then added, "Nick is with Lee in one of the supply buildings."

"What are they doing there?"

"I've no idea."

I found Sam first. He was repairing a shed by the donkey habitat. Tobias and Oliver were hanging out further down in the grassy field.

I told Sam I was here to take a photo for the magazine.

"Animals are a bigger draw than people," he said. "Let's include the donkeys."

As if they knew something was up, Tobias and Oliver began clip-clopping toward us.

"After taking the photo, I asked, "Are you okay? Most people smile when a photo is taken. You didn't."

"Everything is falling apart," he said.

"You mean other than the shed?" I grinned.

"Rumor is we may need to close. Or maybe send some of the animals to other sanctuaries." He rubbed Oliver's head. Tobias pushed his way in-between. "And I can't stop thinking about the murders. Two people are dead. I know I'm a suspect, but I think the police are focused on Declan. Wendy spent a lot of time with him."

"She's studying to be a veterinarian, and he was helping her," I pointed out.

"Yes. But lately it was different."

"How?"

"I saw her leave the veterinary infirmary the day before her murder. She was frowning. Wendy rarely frowned." He paused. "At last, not until recently."

"There could be a million reasons for that." But I made a mental note to ask Declan if there had been a problem.

The last time I took my car up the bumpy path to the storage area, I was afraid I'd wind up with a flat tire, so today I decided to walk. It took nearly twenty-five minutes and much was of my trek was uphill. I was huffing, puffing, and perspiring by the time I arrived. I needed to lose that extra ten pounds.

Unfortunately, Nick and Lee were not in the food storage building, which was air-conditioned with a refrigerated section. They were in the building that housed maintenance equipment, and it was hot.

"You got here just in time. We were about to head back," Nick said when I explained the purpose of my visit. He wiped the sweat off his brow with his hand. "I just finished showing Lee a piece of equipment that needs to be replaced."

Nick chuckled and went on to say, "Lee never takes my word for it. He insists on checking everything himself. Right, Lee?"

"Absolutely. We'll talk later, Nick." He nodded at me, without a smile, and departed.

After I photographed Nick, he said, "I've a batch of donated dog toys in my truck. I'm dropping off a few at the capybara habitat—they love to play with toys. Do you want a lift back?"

"Yes. Thanks." I was still perspiring.

We both climbed in the truck. Once he started the engine, I

said, "I heard the sanctuary is on shaky grounds because of the murders."

"The murders are part of it but not the entire reason. Animal sanctuaries are expensive to operate. Food costs have skyrocketed because of inflation and so have maintenance supplies."

"I get it." I nodded sympathetically. "What do you think will happen?"

He sighed. "Hopefully Gina will use her magic touch and bring in more money. I heard she has another fundraiser planned."

"Do you think she'll raise enough?"

"I've no idea." Nick pulled off the road across from the capybara enclosure. "Gina and Carolyn feel the sooner this case is solved the quicker everything goes back to normal. I think they'll do all they can to resolve this situation. Those two are not only rich, but their families are powerful."

"They have a lot of clout on Long Island and in New York State," I agreed. Rumor was Frank Garone played poker weekly with several political bigwigs. And Frank, supposedly, would do anything for his wife.

"I heard they're pressuring local authorities to make an arrest," Nick said.

"But the arrest would involve a member of their staff. That can't be good publicity," I argued.

"They want this story to go away. Neither Gina nor Caroline wants an investigation hanging over their heads. Once a suspect is arrested, Gina can do damage control."

Public relations 101. Smear the suspect, and paint the accused as a bad penny. Take the focus off the sanctuary.

I sucked in my breath. A quick arrest was what Detective Wolfe was pushing for, too. If he got his way, he would zero in on Declan.

I completed my mission of obtaining photographs of Nick and Sam. I was on my way out when I spied Carolyn Whitcome wandering up the path. Her head was down.

"Carolyn," I called.

She looked up and appeared to force a smile on her face. "How is your story coming?" she asked. "I hope you're portraying the sanctuary in a good light."

"My stories always tell the truth, and the truth is this sanctuary performs an outstanding service. My story will get that across."

"Thank you. We need all the good publicity we can muster." She inhaled deeply before continuing. "I think everything will eventually work out. Gina is a terrific fundraiser, and we are lucky to have Lee as a business manager."

"All your staff seems to do a first-rate job," I said.

"It's more than that. With Lee handling the day-to-day operations, Gina can concentrate on bringing in money. Lee can handle the nuts and bolts—the daily grind. In lots of not-for-profit organizations, the director has to do both."

I remembered the comment Wendy made suggesting Gina should be more hands on. I also recalled Professor Munch's remarks about Gina's less than stellar skills in budgeting.

Carolyn appeared to gaze at the surroundings. "I also think once an arrest is made, things will get back to normal."

"Arrest? Have the police made any progress?"

"I heard they brought Declan Carr into headquarters for questioning this morning."

"Into headquarters," I repeated, weakly. Questioning was one thing. But bringing someone into headquarters for that questioning was a bad sign. How imminent was an arrest?

At that moment my phone beeped. It was a text from Jason with the autopsy findings in Wendy's death. My stomach churned. I was sure this was part of the reason Declan was in

an interrogation room right now.
The cause of death was etorphine.

CHAPTER 54

"That was my fifth coffee," Abby said. "I feel like a squirrel on steroids."

I laughed. "This is the morning breakfast rush hour. We've a better chance of engaging in conversation with wait staff if we order something."

Declan was not arrested yesterday but had been told not to leave town. According to Fox, the police were waiting for the district attorney to return from vacation later this week. This way, he could hold a press conference where he would make the announcement charging Declan with the murders.

Today, Abby and I were checking out the diners, hoping to discover where Wendy had been the morning of her murder. So far, no luck.

"I'd like food along with my coffee."

"We'll get something to eat at this place," I replied to my daughter as I pulled into the Oakridge Diner parking lot. "This is our last stop today. If no one recognizes the photos here, we've reached a dead end."

"This diner looks different than the others," Abby noted, hopping out of the car.

The five previous diners were large and modern. This place, which on the outside resembled an oversized trailer, looked as if it dated back to the 1950s. As we stepped inside, I quickly observed the retro décor—Formica tables, black and white checkered wall tiles, and a large jukebox in the corner. There was a long counter with stools and fewer than a dozen booths.

We no sooner sat down when a server handed us menus. She was short and stocky with curly red hair and a smattering of freckles. A heart tattoo occupied a large portion of her left forearm.

"Coffee?" she asked. We nodded and she poured. Her name tag identified her as Wilma. "I'll be back in a few minutes to take your order."

Once she disappeared into the kitchen, Abby said, "She appears to be the only server besides the man behind the counter."

"If Wendy was meeting someone, they would want the privacy of a booth. Let's hope Wilma worked here last Monday and that Wendy was a customer."

When Wilma returned, I ordered blueberry pancakes, and Abby chose an omelet.

"If you have a moment, I wonder if you recognize the woman in this photograph," I asked, pulling out the picture of Wendy.

Suddenly, Wilma's mouth opened in surprise. "I saw this picture on the news too. Isn't she the woman who was murdered?"

I nodded. "Did you ever see her in here?"

"You mean in the diner?" Wilma nodded, emphatically. "Yes. She was here last week. I remember now because she acted so skittish."

"What do you mean?"

"She was nervous and distracted. She was constantly glancing all over the place. And every time I approached her table, she was fiddling with her necklace."

"Her necklace," I repeated. "What did it look like?"

"Gold chain with the letter W. I remember because that's my

initial too. W for Wilma." She pointed to her name tag.

I realized if Wendy wore the necklace on the morning of her murder, it meant she lost it later that day.

In the storage facility.

Why was she there?

"Was someone with her here at the diner?" Abby asked Wilma.

"The man she sat with had arrived first, and he asked for a table in the back." Wilma paused and added, "He was a tea drinker." She said that as if he asked for pickle juice.

"When did the woman in the photo arrive?" I asked.

"About fifteen minutes later."

"Do you think you would recognize a picture of the man?" I asked as I reached into my tote bag and grabbed the photos of the three suspects.

She nodded.

My heard skipped a beat as I whipped out the photographs of Nick, Sam, and Declan.

"No," Wilma said. "None of those pictures are of him."

"You're sure?"

She nodded. "The man I saw had jet black hair, like the three men in the photos. But this man's skin was fair, almost pale. I remember because I thought he probably sunburns like me."

Wilma left and Abby shook her head, "So who did Wendy meet?"

"I've no idea. According to the time of Wendy's death, only Declan, Nick, and Sam were in the sanctuary when she was killed. I was sure her morning breakfast meeting had to be with one of those three."

I sipped my coffee. "Even Lee, who has an alibi, couldn't be the person Wendy met. He has sandy blond hair. And it couldn't be Gina because Maureen said she was meeting with a man."

"Maybe Wendy's diner meeting had nothing to do with her

murder."

I shook my head. "Wilma said Wendy appeared nervous. My gut tells me this is all related."

"Maybe her killer had an accomplice, and that's who she met?"

"This case is impossible—"

"Here you go," Wilma interrupted when she returned with our meals.

"I may need to talk to you again," I said. "Are you here every morning?

"Usually, but I won't be next week because of our summer vacation schedule. The cook's daughter is filling in for breakfast and early lunch. I've got the dinner and late night shift. You can reach me here after three in the afternoon."

Wilma handed me handful of syrup packets for my pancakes and added, "I remember something else about that woman in the photo. When she entered the diner, the man called her over to his table."

"Why is that significant?" Abby asked with a puzzled look on her face.

"Because, at first, I don't think she recognized him."

CHAPTER 55

"Why wouldn't Wendy recognize the man she was meeting?" I asked Abby as we hopped in the car and drove away from the diner.

"It fits the theory of an accomplice," Abby said. "If more than one person is involved, maybe this other person doesn't work at the sanctuary, and never met Wendy."

"Then what would be the motive? I'm convinced the murders involve wrongdoings at the sanctuary. How does that fit with an outside accomplice?" I rubbed my head.

Dozens of ideas squirreled around in my mind. But none made any sense.

When I dropped my daughter off at her house, I went inside to use her bathroom—I'd consumed a lot of coffee this morning. As I was about to leave, my phone trilled. The name *Nora* flashed across the screen. That was Maureen McDermott's sister.

"I didn't know who else to contact," she said. "No one from the sanctuary has returned my calls, so I hoped maybe you could help."

"Is something wrong?" I asked.

"Wrong? Oh, no. It's just that I've been clearing out my sister's condo and found about a dozen pictures of Maureen with her animals. They're good photographs. I thought the sanctuary might want them."

"I'm sure they'd love them," I said, although I had no idea if they would or wouldn't. "Why don't I pick them up from you and take them there."

"Great. I'll be here most of the day. I'll text you the address."

I finished the call and stashed my phone back in my bag.

"What are you up to, Mom?" Abby asked.

"I'm headed to Maureen McDermott's condo." I told her about my conversation with Nora. "I'm sure the police checked out Maureen's place, but maybe they missed evidence because they didn't realize it had anything to do with her murder. While there, I'll investigate."

Abby grinned. "A long shot but worth a try."

Maureen lived in a luxury condo that I assumed she purchased when she made mega bucks as an attorney.

The doorman phoned Nora and got the okay to send me up. I headed for the elevator. Nora was waiting for me at the door to her sister's unit.

"It's a good thing I'm a teacher and have the summer off," Nora said as she led me through a spacious living room which overlooked the Long Island Sound with views of Connecticut. "Otherwise, I don't know when I'd find the time to get this all done."

We made our way into the bedroom where clothes were strewn across the bed, and several cartons sealed with tape occupied the floor.

"The photos of the sanctuary animals are in there," she said, pointing to a manila envelope atop the dresser.

Also on the dresser top were three photos of Maureen with a man. I assumed he was her late husband.

"I guess I'll throw those out," Nora said when she spied me glancing at the pictures. "I feel terrible but what can I do? I never met her husband, but I think she really loved him."

"I'm putting the condo up for sale too." she continued. "The real estate agent said places sell faster if they're void of personal effects. Those pictures are the only personal items here, except for a few pieces of jewelry."

I felt it was time to change the subject. "Do you mind if I look around the condo. I'm hoping there might be a clue to her murder that the police overlooked."

"Go ahead. But I've emptied out all the dresser drawers in this room."

"Did you find any papers or journals?"

Nora shook her head. "All she had were clothes."

I quickly checked my surroundings. Doesn't she have a desk?"

"That's in her office—the room to the left. But the police took her computer. I think the only items left in her desk were pens, pencils, and stationery—that sort of thing."

I made my way into Maureen's home office. The furnishings were Spartan—a desk, chair, and a file cabinet.

I peeked first into the file cabinet. It was stuffed with manila folders.

"The police didn't want these?" I asked.

"The police looked at the files but said nothing was relevant. Detective Wolfe told me each folder dealt with a case back when Maureen worked as a lawyer. These cases were probably on her computer, but it's in keeping with Maureen's general lack of trust to make hard copies of everything."

The information may be old, but still, could there be a connection the police missed?

"I'd like to read these files. What are you planning to do with them?"

"I was going to shred them. If I let you see them, isn't that a violation of attorney/client privilege?"

"Neither of us is an attorney," I said, although I didn't know if that absolved us. "But I will keep everything confidential unless it relates to Maureen's murder. If it does, I'll contact the police."

"I don't know." I heard the hesitancy in Nora's voice. "I guess it would be okay."

"Thanks. I'll take them home and read them tonight."

I grabbed the folders and placed them on the top of the desk for later. Then I pulled open the drawers to check if anything remained. Nora was right. Nothing was there except some stationery supplies. But as I glanced down, I spotted a wastepaper basket next to the desk and noticed it contained a few scraps of paper. I bent down and grabbed them.

Most of the papers were discarded junk mail, including a flyer for a computer repair service and two fast food take-out menus. But one item caught my eye. Scrawled on notepaper was the following question: *How much fish is needed?*

"Nora, do you know what this means?" I showed her the note.

Nora examined the paper and frowned. "I have no idea. Maureen didn't like to entertain, so I doubt if she was planning a dinner party."

"Maybe it has to do with fish purchased by the sanctuary," I said. I stuffed the note in my bag and continued searching the house. Finally, I said, "I've looked in every room except the kitchen. I'm going to check there."

"The cabinets are empty." Nora followed me into the room. "The cartons on the floor are her dishes, glasses, and so on. "I'll see if my daughter wants them. Otherwise I'll donate them to a soup kitchen."

I spotted a piece of lined yellow paper on the kitchen counter. I grabbed it.

"Oh, that's my shopping list," Nora said, "On my way home. I'm stopping at a farm stand a few miles from here. Their fruits and vegetables are delicious."

I glanced at the note. On it was scribbled:

Peaches
Blueberries
Melons

I recalled Nick telling me the other day how much bears like peaches. Suddenly, something struck a chord. I realized the first two words on Nora's shopping list began with a *P and B.*

Those were also the first letters listed on the second page in Wendy's notebook.

Could the *P* and *B* in Wendy's list stand for produce—peaches and blueberries? Those were foods that many animal species ate.

I'd taken photos with my phone of the lists in Wendy's notebook. I checked it now and discovered the letters *P* and *B* were followed by *G, A,* and *B.* I thought about the fruits I saw at the sanctuary that were fed to the animals. In addition to peaches and blueberries, there were grapes, apples, and bananas.

G for grapes, A for apples, and B for bananas.

I began putting things together.

The letters on the chart in Wendy's notebook.

The scrap of paper with the question: *How much fish is needed?*

Carolyn's comment to Gina the other day about the high cost of food.

Maureen had discovered something happening at the sanctuary. And I think it had to do with food purchases.

CHAPTER 56

I grabbed the old case files and the folder with the animal photos, scooted out of Nora's condo, and continued on my way, driving a little faster than I should. I didn't want to be late for my next appointment. It was with Jake Spano—Maureen McDermott's former private investigator.

When I pulled into the parking lot of Jake's office, it wasn't at all what I expected. Perhaps it was my *mystery noir* image of private eyes, but I envisioned a gumshoe working out of a ramshackle building, next to a bar in the worst part of town.

Jake's office was located in a modern glass and steel high-rise in one of the major business corridors on Long Island. According to the lobby directory, he shared this building with several other entities including a law firm, title company, insurance agency, dental group and proctology office. Spano Investigations took up the entire fourth floor.

I settled down in the waiting room and watched the local news on a widescreen television until the receptionist announced that Mister Spano would see me now. As I stepped into his private office, I was again surprised. I needed to stop watching those Sam Spade movies.

I had pictured a down and out, somewhat sleazy private eye with a cigarette dangling from his mouth. With his brown hair graying at the temples, horn rimmed glasses, and charcoal pinstripe suit, Jake Spano looked more like a banker. He motioned me to a chair facing his desk.

"When we talked on the phone, you said you wanted to see me about Maureen McDermott. What is this about?" he asked.

I explained what information I was seeking.

He frowned. "The work I do is confidential."

"Your client is dead. The subject of one of your investigations may be the murderer."

His eyes narrowed into slits as he drummed his fingers on his desk. He appeared to be thinking about what to do.

"I'm sure Maureen would want her killer brought to justice," I added.

He grinned. "That's true. Okay. Ask me your questions, and I'll try to help."

I pulled out a photo and slapped it down on his desk.

"This is Wendy Wu. Did you ever investigate her for Maureen? Or do you know if Maureen had any connection to her?"

"The name isn't familiar, and I don't recognize the photograph. But I investigated lots of people for Maureen. Let me pull up her files and check."

He scrolled down and shook his head. "No investigation was ever opened on a Wendy Wu."

"Could she be part of an investigation not under her name? Maybe she was a victim or a witness."

"I can't be sure without rereading all of Maureen's case files."

I didn't think he was about to do that. I reached across his desk and handed him a list. "Do you recognize any of these names?"

Gina Garone

Declan Carr

Nick Lamonica

Sam Garcia

Lee Adler

"This one I don't need to look up," he said, pointing to Nick Lamonica's name. "Boy! Did she rake him over the coals?"

We chatted about Nick, but Jake didn't tell me anything I didn't know.

"Let's quickly look up the others on your list," he suggested as he scrolled down his computer.

"I investigated a Regina Carr a long time ago and discovered her family included a nephew named Declan. He was a young boy at the time, and there was nothing on him. But a few months ago, Maureen asked me to check him out again. I found he had a drinking problem in college but appeared to have conquered it."

Jake sat back in his swivel chair and chuckled. "Maureen was annoyed that he was no longer under the influence of the *drinking demon*. She asked me to dig deeper and I did. He's been sober for more than seven years. Maureen wasn't happy. She really wanted me to find dirt."

Jake continued scrolling. "I've nothing on Sam Garcia."

That's because Maureen didn't need to dig up dirt on him, I realized. She destroyed his family business with mail order roaches. So far, I wasn't getting any new information.

Jake paused. "Those two are recent." He pointed to the first and last names on the list. "Gina Garone and Lee Adler."

"How recent? How did they come up?"

"A short time ago, Maureen phoned and asked me to investigate the sanctuary finances. I keep a forensic accountant on retainer, and she wanted me to have him go over the sanctuary's books. The sanctuary is a non-profit, so their books are public record. Maureen said if I found discrepancies I needed to check out the finances of Gina and Lee."

"What did you discover?"

"Nothing. When Maureen called, I told her my firm was in the midst of a big case and couldn't start for at least another week. She was okay with that. But she died five days after she called me. We never started the investigation."

He paused as he leaned forward and formed a steeple with his fingers. "The day she died, I received a check as a retainer. I never cashed it."

"What specifically was she looking for?"

"She didn't say. She told me when my firm was ready to investigate, she would sit down with me and the accountant I have on staff. She'd explain it then."

On a hunch I showed him the photos I'd taken of the letters and numbers in Wendy's notebook.

"Have you ever seen these?"

"Nope." He shook his head.

"Thank you." I rose from my chair. There was nothing more I had to ask now.

He stood up, and we shook hands. As I departed, he said, "Maureen McDermott always wanted to know where the bodies were buried. It wasn't difficult, because in many cases, she was the one who buried them."

CHAPTER 57

Clara called the next morning with good news and bad news. The good news was great news—Olivia was out of her coma.

The bad news—Clara didn't know when Olivia would be well enough to return to the office. In the meantime, Griffin DeMott, our temporary editor, was still in charge, and he had called a meeting for tomorrow.

I spent the rest of the day at home reading Maureen's old law case files—the ones from her condo—but I found nothing remotely connected to the sanctuary. Since my magazine story was due by the end of next week, I was racing the clock. Something sinister was going on, and it was bad enough to cause two murders. I was sure the murders had to do with sanctuary purchases. But would I solve the case in time to meet my magazine's deadline? More importantly, would I solve it before Declan was arrested?

I wondered if I would solve it at all.

That night, I tossed and turned. It wasn't Matt's snoring keeping me awake. Dozens of thoughts swirled around in my mind. I finally fell asleep. When I awoke I had a plan of action.

Later that day, as I swung open the door to the *Animal Advocate* office, I felt those spiders crawling around in my intestines.

Clara was sitting at the front desk. Her smile was gone. We nodded to each other. I grabbed a mug of coffee and scooted off to my cubicle.

The staff meeting wasn't until ten. I had nearly an hour to do more investigating. The first step of my plan of action was to scrutinize the sanctuary's expenditures line by line.

Before writing the first draft of my magazine story, I'd read the narrative portion of the sanctuary's annual report, but I hadn't checked the financial statistics listed in the back. I would do that now and fill in the figures where needed. I didn't want to include too many numbers as most readers would find that boring, and my article was a human interest story, focusing on the animals. But good journalism required that I include some statistics to back up my narrative.

I decided to check the financial figures now. I pulled out a copy of the annual report Lee gave me when I interviewed him. I started reading. Suddenly, things began to make sense.

On the first page of the financial section of the report was a chart that read:

	Donated	Purchased	Needed
Meats	10,000 p	5,000 p	15,000 p
Fish	15,000p	30,000 p	45,000p
Produce	40,000p	30,000 p	70,000p

I pulled out my phone and went to the photo I'd taken of the chart in Wendy's notebook.

	D	P	N	
M	10,000p	10,000 p	15,000 p	(5,000)
F	15,000 p	40,000p	45,000 p	(10,000)

"This is it," I mumbled, excitedly.

D, P, and *N* stood for donated, purchased, and needed. *M* meant meat, and *F* meant fish. I was pretty sure the *p* after each number stood for pounds.

On the second page, Wendy had listed a bunch of letters, which I was sure corresponded with different fruits. Did the question mark after each letter refer to the amount ordered?

As I compared the chart in Wendy's notebook with the one in the annual report, I noted the numbers were different. In the annual report, the donated and purchased amount added up to the exact amount in the needed column.

But in the chart scribbled in Wendy's notebook, the combined amount of donated and purchased exceeded the amount needed—meat by 5,000 pounds and fish by 10,000 pounds.

Was someone cooking the books?

I quickly phoned Declan and told him what I had discovered.

"I need to find out which chart is correct," I said, although I was sure it was the one in Wendy's notebook. But I had to make certain. "I need to see Lee's files."

"Not possible."

"We could go at night—"

"No. We'd be caught on the security camera at the sanctuary entrance. Neither of us needs a breaking and entering charge. But I do have an idea."

"What?"

"The Seafarer's Cooperative donates a certain amount of fish each year, but it's not enough for all our needs. I always thought we purchase whatever else we require from them, but now I'm not sure. Ask the manager at the cooperative for the exact numbers. Say it's for your magazine story."

"That could work," I said as a thought popped in my mind. I remembered my first day at the sanctuary when Maureen angrily questioned Nick about changing the food order for the capybara.

"Who determines how much food and what type of food is ordered?" I asked.

"The keeper in charge makes the recommendation. But the ultimate decision is made by the head animal keeper. After that, it needs to be approved by Lee or Gina, but it always is."

The head animal keeper. Nick Lamonica.

Could Nick be over-ordering and selling the extra? As someone who spent his adult life in the animal world, he would know where to peddle it?

"Text me the contact information for the Seafarer's Cooperative," I said to Declan. "I'll get in touch with them."

I said good-bye to Declan as Clara barged into my cubicle.

"You need to go to the conference room for the meeting," she said.

I glanced at my watch. "It's nine fifty-five. I have five minutes."

"You know how he is about punctuality."

Clara was right. I rose from my chair and trailed her to the meeting room. The rest of the staff was there. I'd never seen gloomier faces. It looked like a group of prisoners waiting to face the firing squad.

Within seconds, Griffin DeMott sauntered into the room.

"Let's get to business. How many of you have sold an ad?"

I'd convinced my husband to advertise in the magazine. *Animal Advocate* was read by animal lovers, many of whom had companion animals. A large portion of subscribers lived on Long Island. He might attract business from the ad.

Griffin went around the room and asked each of us individually. The senior reporter sold to a travel company specializing in African photo safaris. The editorial assistant had convinced an animal physic to advertise. So far, everyone had sold an ad—until he came to Clara.

Clara shook her head. "I'm sorry. I haven't been able to sell anything."

"Our advertisers pay your salary, Ms. Schultheis," he said, referring to Clara by her surname. "You appear to be the only one here who wasn't able to perform this simple task. We can't keep people on the payroll who don't support the team,"

I sucked in my breath. I loved my job—it was my life's dream to become a journalist, and I left a tenured teaching position to pursue this dream. But Clara needed this job financially.

"Excuse me," I interrupted. "Clara hasn't sold any ads yet, but she has a deal in progress." I rummaged through my brain until an idea popped up.

"She's in talks with a cruise line that goes to Alaska," I said. I needed to stall for time. Perhaps I could then help Clara secure an ad.

"What cruise line, Clara," Griffin asked, staring directly at her.

Clara looked like a deer caught in the headlights. My chatty friend was speechless. I had to say something.

As the name of different cruise lines flashed through my mind, my thoughts were interrupted by a familiar voice echoing in the room.

"I only heard the tail end of the conversation, but I don't like what I heard," the voice said.

It was Olivia.

Griffin scowled. "I'm in charge—"

"Not anymore. "I've been released from the hospital, and I'm ready to get back to work. I've talked to corporate. They want you back in the main office. If you haven't received an email from them yet, you will at any moment."

Griffin pulled out his phone. As he scrolled down, his scowl deepened. It was apparent the email had been sent.

"This is a big mistake on their part. You may be a good journalist, but magazines today are all about the bottom line. You and your magazine won't make it."

"Yes, we will," Olivia said as he stormed out of the room. I smiled. We had Olivia back.

CHAPTER 58

When I returned to my house, I noticed no one had brought in the mail. By no one, I meant Matt, who had been home for several hours.

I carried the mail into the kitchen, assuming it was the usual assortment of junk solicitations and bills. I placed the mail on the kitchen table and returned to it after I let Brandy and Archie out.

A large manila envelope caught my attention. There was no return address, I slit it open and pulled out a photograph.

My hands began shaking.

"Mom, what's wrong?" Abby stepped into the house. She apparently saw the expression of horror on my face.

"What's going on?" she asked again.

"I got this in the mail." I thrust the photo into her hands. It was a picture of Abby jogging in the local park. Her hand was on the back of her neck as if she were scratching or rubbing something.

Attached to the photograph was a note that read:

You probably thought it was a wasp.
It wasn't.
It was a dart.
It came from a blowgun.
You felt a sting—a little pinch.

It was only a dart.
But next time, it could be covered in poison.
You'll never know where or when I'll strike.
But I'll make a deal.
If you stay away from the sanctuary murders
I'll disappear

"I'm calling Detective Fox." I grabbed my phone.

"I'm texting Jason."

Thirty minutes later, Detective Fox and Jason were in my kitchen. Matt was there, too. When I first showed him the photo and note, he turned ashen.

Luckily, my mother was out to dinner with friends tonight.

"This must have been taken last Thursday," Abby said. "It was early evening, right after work. I thought I was stung by a wasp."

I nodded. "I remember. You stopped here later, and you rubbed your neck a few times."

"Kristy, you need to stop this investigation," Matt said.

"No Dad. It's too important. We can't give into threats."

"Can't you prohibit a civilian from interfering in a police investigation?" Matt asked Detective Fox.

Before Fox could respond, I spoke up, "Maybe I should stop. Abby's safety is my top priority." I paused. "But I don't understand why they targeted Abby instead of me. She's been with me a few times, but not a lot."

"You just said why," Fox answered. "You wouldn't back down if the threat was to you. But you're ready to stop to protect your daughter."

"How could the killer know about my jogging?" Abby asked.

"Do you ever post about it on social media?"

"Never. Sometimes I'll post photos when I'm out with friends.

But I've never had a picture taken when I'm jogging."

"Do your friends know you jog?" Detective Fox asked.

"Yes. You don't think this is a friend, do you?"

"Does Declan Carr know you jog?"

"That's ridiculous. There's no way—"

Fox held up his hands. "I'm not saying Declan did this. But it's possible he talked about you at the sanctuary."

"But even if he mentioned having a friend who jogs, who would know besides Declan that Abby is Kristy's daughter?" Matt asked.

"I'm afraid several staff members know," I said. "The first day I was at the sanctuary, I ran into Declan. Gina and Lee were there, and I told them Declan was a friend of my daughter.

"Since they both have alibis for the time Wendy was killed, Gina and Lee are not among the murder suspects," Fox reminded us. "What about Nick or Sam?"

"I don't know if Sam is aware, but Nick knows. I mentioned Abby to him when he told me about his wife's job with Omega Animal Grooming Supplies. I told him my daughter was a veterinarian. I said she worked at my husband's veterinary hospital."

"If he knew where she worked, it would be easy for him to stalk her." Fox glanced down at the photo. "You said this was taken in the early evening?"

Abby nodded. "I like to jog when the sun is still out, and I'm not a morning person. I usually change clothes at the veterinary hospital after I finish my shift and then go straight to the park."

"So, if he was stalking you at work, he easily could have trailed you to the park. Do you usually jog at the same time?"

Abby nodded. "Three days a week."

"You need to stop that for a while. Stay away from isolated spots. This maniac won't take a chance in a crowd. It's too easy to be spotted and he could hit a bystander."

"Okay. I can forgo jogging for now, but I don't want my mom to stop her investigation."

"I don't like this. The police should be handling this case." Matt ran his hand through his thinning hair.

"But that's not going to happen," Abby replied. "Detective Wolfe is convinced Declan is the killer. He's ordered Detective Fox to stop investigating on his own. Mom needs to continue."

"I'm still investigating on my days off," Detective Fox added.

"There may not be time," I said. "We're racing the clock, and Wolfe is watching you like a hawk. But I have an idea. What if the killer THINKS I've stopped investigating?"

I had everyone's attention.

"What do you mean?" Jason asked. He had been quiet up until now, but I noticed he took in every word that was said.

"I can let it be known that I only have to add a few more details, and my story on the sanctuary will be done. I'll say I received a new magazine assignment, and I'll be moving on with no time to continue looking into the murders. This way, everyone will think I've stopped investigating, but, of course, I'll continue."

"That should work," Abby agreed.

"It's too dangerous," Matt argued. "If the killer realizes you're still snooping—"

"That won't happen. I'll be discreet."

"I agree with Matt," Detective Fox said. "I'm going to ask you to let the police handle this case, but I know you and Abby are not going to listen." He sighed. "Be careful."

CHAPTER 59

I would have to be careful about how I asked for the information needed. I was headed to the Seafarer's Cooperative to ascertain how much fish the sanctuary purchased from them and how much was donated. My questions needed to be casual, and I had to give the impression that my focus was to show how generous the organization was with their contributions.

I could tell I was close to my destination. As I sped along the coast road with my car windows open, I inhaled the salt air. Now that salt air was mixed with the strong odor of fish. I was nearing the docks.

I spotted the huge sign that read *Seafarer's Cooperative—Entrance*. I slowed down as I drove into the gravel parking lot. I hopped out of the car and made my way to the pier, which was directly in front of me. To my left was a steel warehouse and to my right a small clapboard house.

Only three boats were currently docked. They probably delivered their morning catch and had not gone out again. The bulk of the fishing vessels would be back later in the day, so I figured this would be a relatively quiet time—a good time to talk.

A tall, skinny teenager with carrot-colored hair and a face covered with freckles was washing one of the boats as I approached.

"Good morning. I'm looking for Paul Conroy," I said. Declan had told me that Paul ran the Seafarer's Cooperative.

"He's not here." The freckled faced boy continued washing the boat.

"Do you know when he will be?"

"Sometime later."

"Can you be more specific?"

"Huh?"

"In an hour? Two hours? Tomorrow? I can wait a bit, but if he won't be here until much later, I'll come back."

"Don't know." He shrugged. "He could be here in ten minutes or at the end of the day."

I sighed and decided to wait in my car a little longer, hoping he would arrive soon.

"Do you want to see his assistant," the boy called as I began walking away. "He's here."

I turned around. "Sure. Perhaps he could help."

"He's in the house. His name is Fred."

The clapboard house was tiny. I swung open the door and found myself facing two wooden desks both with a chair behind them and a folding chair in front. Between each desk was an old-fashioned electric fan. There was no air conditioning. A long table hugged the right wall, and two metal file cabinets were on the left. On each desk was a computer, appearing out of place in this building which looked as if it hadn't been updated in sixty years.

Sitting behind one of the desks was a man with a weather-beaten face and a muscular build, indicative of someone who spent lots of time performing outdoor labor. I told him I was a reporter doing a story on the Happy Place Animal Sanctuary. I asked him to explain how the Seafarer's Cooperative worked.

He sat back. "Fishing fleets bring in their catches, and we sell in bulk. That way we can get the best price. About seventy percent of the fishing industry out here belongs. The other thirty percent are independent."

"I understand you donate seafood to the animal sanctuary, too."

He nodded. "We do. We give to several causes. Each month, we also provide fish to a local homeless shelter."

"Can you tell me exactly how much you contributed to the sanctuary and how much you've sold to them?"

"Not off the top of my head." He smiled, showing yellow teeth. Judging by the tobacco smell in the room, I assumed he was smoker. "Let me look it up."

Looks can be deceiving. I expected him to head for the metal cabinets, but instead he turned toward the computer on his desk. His fingers moved quickly across the keyboard, and in minutes he had the information I needed,

"Here we go. We donated fifteen thousand pounds of fish, and the sanctuary purchased thirty thousand pounds. This includes clams and crabs too."

This was the amount listed in the annual report—not the amount in Wendy's notebook. Her notebook listed the amount purchased as 40,000 pounds.

"Do you know if the sanctuary buys seafood anywhere else?"

He shook his head. "I don't know for sure."

As I pondered what to ask next, the fan blew a paper off Fred's desk. That jogged my memory. During my first interview with Lee Adler, a bill for fish had fallen off his desk. The name on the top of this bill had not been the Seafarer's Cooperative. It was the Relda Animal Food and Supply Corporation. I'd forgotten that until now.

Perhaps the extra fish listed in Wendy's chart came from the Relda Corporation.

"Are you familiar with the Relda Corporation?" I asked.

"Nope. Never heard of them."

I couldn't think of anything else to ask, but I needed to find out more about Relda.

Back home, I searched on the internet and found nothing. The Relda Corporation appeared to be a ghost.

"Lee should be able to tell me about this company," I mumbled, as I rose from my chair. Archie, who had been resting on my foot, grumbled. I think I woke him up.

I glanced at my watch. Matt and I were going out tonight, and it was time for me to get ready. I climbed upstairs, rummaged through my closet, and finally selected a sleeveless, sea-green sheath dress.

I headed to the bathroom to take a quick shower. But before I got there, I grabbed a piece of paper and jotted down the word Relda followed by questions for Lee whom I planned to reach tomorrow.

I absentmindedly held onto the note as I made my way to the bathroom. Rather than go back to the bedroom and place it on the dresser, I laid it on the vanity in front of the mirror. I undressed and stepped into the shower.

When I emerged from the shower, I was taken aback. As I picked up the note, I could see its reflection in the mirror. The reflection, of course, was backward. Although the letters were also in a backward position, I could make out one of the words, and it sent a shiver up my spine.

RELDA backwards spelled ADLER.

CHAPTER 60

"There's no way this is a coincidence," I said on the phone to Abby. "Lee Adler has to be the person behind the Relda Corporation."

"You're right. You discovered a clue that could lead to a scandal at the sanctuary."

"Scandal, yes. But I'm not any closer in figuring out who killed Maureen and Wendy. I believe the same person killed them both. And Lee has an ironclad alibi for the time of Wendy's death."

"What about the accomplice theory? Maybe she met with Lee—"

"He couldn't be the mystery man," I interrupted as I thought back to the server's reaction at the diner.

"How do you know that? You only showed Wilma a photo of Nick, Sam and Declan. You never showed her Lee's picture."

"Wilma described the mystery man as having fair skin and black hair. Lee has light sandy blond hair. And if Lee was the one, I'm sure she would have mentioned his glasses, too."

"I still think discovering the Relda Corporation is a huge breakthrough."

"I do too. And Lee is somehow involved."

Have you conducted any research on Relda?"

"There's nothing on social media. Tomorrow I plan to go to

the sanctuary and see if I can discover more."

"Is that the only way? That's got to arouse suspicion."

"Only if I involve Lee. I plan to get the information from other sources. Once I do, I'll turn everything over to Detective Fox."

"But someone may tell Lee about your inquiries—"

"I'll be discreet." I interrupted. "When I arrive at the sanctuary tomorrow, I'll let it be known that my deadline is Monday. I'll announce that since the police murder investigation is still ongoing, it will be too late to include, so my story will focus on the sanctuary's operation and the wonderful work it does."

"Let's hope everyone believes you."

"As a former teacher, I know how to ask questions without causing suspicion."

"True." Abby chuckled. "When I was a teenager, you always knew what I was doing, but I never suspected you were aware." She paused. "Just be careful. Lee may have an alibi for Wendy's death but he doesn't for the murder of Maureen. If he's working with an accomplice, you're putting yourself in danger."

"Of course, I'll be careful." I thought back to the picture of Abby and the accompanying note. "I would never put you at risk."

After finishing our conversation, I began dressing for the evening. Matt and I were headed to the community theatre tonight for the official opening of *The Murder of Lord Kent,* the British mystery starring my friend Alicia Layne.

Perhaps watching an old-fashioned murder mystery would clear my mind and help me come up with an idea.

The play was superb, but it didn't clear my head or give me any ideas. After the curtain call, Matt and I strolled into the lobby. The theatre owner was hosting a wine and cheese reception for ticket holders and the cast.

I was taking my first sip of white wine when Alicia Layne made her grand entrance. She was no longer dressed as Lady Kent, the character she played in the show. She now wore a pink and purple caftan with a matching turban, and she sported rings on eight of her ten fingers.

"You were wonderful," I said.

"I never guessed you were the murderess," Matt added.

"How about you, Kristy?" Alicia winked. "Did you guess it?"

"No. I didn't recognize you as Lady Kent when you were disguised as the old peddler woman who poisons Lord Kent."

"Disguises are amazing," Alicia said. "It's so easy to transform your look into something completely different."

I recalled my mother's statement the day after she followed Austin and Mille Briggs. She said they wouldn't recognize her because she wore a wig. An image flooded my mind.

I turned to my husband. "Matt, I think the mystery man at the diner could be Lee Adler. He's fair skinned. The black hair could be a wig."

Matt narrowed his eyes. "But why would he do that?"

"Because he knew the murder would be in the news along with Wendy's picture. He couldn't take the chance that someone from the diner recognized him as the man with Wendy and called the police. Lee had to disguise himself."

"I guess that makes sense."

"Before I do anything else, I'm taking a photo of Lee. Do you remember Abby's friend Julia, the artist? I going to ask her if she can draw a picture of Lee from the photo, but change his hair to black and omit the glasses. Then I'll go back to the diner and show the drawing to Wilma."

Matt furrowed his brows.

"Don't you think I'm on the right track?" I asked.

"I'm afraid you are. Please be careful."

CHAPTER 61

When I pulled into the sanctuary lot, I recognized Lee Adler's car.

"Good. He's here," I mumbled.

I stepped into the administration building. The doors to both Gina's and Lee's offices were shut.

I scooted to Lee's office and knocked, hoping he was inside.

"Come in."

The expression on his face as I stepped into his room was both surprised and annoyed. "I thought you were Gina," he said, scowling.

"I won't take up much of your time. I need to photograph you for my magazine story."

His scowl deepened.

"I won't take long. Remember, your board chair, Carolyn Whitcome, wants all staff to cooperate." She hadn't specifically said that, but it was probably true.

"Please make it fast."

After photographing Lee, I said, "I have a quick question. Where does the sanctuary get its seafood?"

"The Seafarer's Cooperative."

"No place else?"

"We may occasionally place small orders with another company, but I can't remember offhand. If we did, it would have been for an insignificant amount."

He moved forward in his chair, grabbing the edge of his desk with his hands. "Any more questions?" His eyes became slits, and he reminded me of a tiger ready to pounce.

I thanked him for his time and left as he returned to his computer. Once outside the building, I phoned my daughter.

"I want your friend Julia to draw a picture for me based on a photograph, but I need her to change it slightly by taking off the glasses and giving the subject a different hair coloring," I said.

"No problem."

"I need it quickly?"

"How quickly?"

"In a day or two."

"I'll ask her. As long as she's not working on another project and has the time, she can do it. What's this about?"

I explained my theory and texted the photo. I had no doubt as to Julia's artistic skills. The question was, did she have the time?

I was about to head toward the parking lot when I spotted Gina strutting toward the building.

"I'm returning from a meeting with the caterer for Monday night's fundraiser," she said, after we greeted each other. "It's a Wolf Howl. Guests get a private walking tour of the sanctuary at night. Several of our animals are nocturnal and more active then. But the main attraction is listening to the wolves. The howling is simply chilling."

As what appeared to be an afterthought, she added. "At the end of the event, we're having a dessert table."

"Sounds fabulous. I'd love to attend. I could mention it in my article."

Gina hesitated but then nodded. "You can come as my guest."

"Thanks. That should finish it up too. I have a new assignment starting next week, so Monday night will be the last time you'll see me."

"I'm glad you're almost done with your story." Gina appeared to relax.

"I have one more question," I said, segueing into what I needed to ask. "Does the sanctuary buy many products from the Relda Corporation?"

She scratched her head. "The name sounds familiar. Maybe we purchase from them, but I can't remember."

"Where do you get your seafood?"

"Seafarer's Cooperative. They donate a substantial amount, so I insist we buy from them too."

"Seafarer is the only place? Are you sure you don't get some from the Relda Corporation?"

Gina shrugged. "I don't recall. I only make sure we support our donors and buy something from them. As I mentioned before, I'm not a bean counter. Whoever else we buy from is up to Lee."

"But as director, don't you need to give final approval on purchases?"

She winced. "Technically, yes. But if Lee is okay with it, I'm usually good. I don't have the time with my public relations and fundraising activities."

"I understand."

Gina obviously signed off on everything Lee approved, but she paid little attention to what she was signing off on.

Gina made her way into the administration building. I was about to leave when I spotted Declan heading toward me. He looked despondent.

"Any news?" I asked.

He shook his head. "I don't like what I'm hearing. Nick and Sam both think I'm going to be arrested this weekend."

"Nick and Sam are the other two suspects," I reminded him. "And it's all rumor. You know how rumors take on a life of their own."

He sighed. "Meanwhile, the hydraulic lift on my examining table isn't working. I've got to talk to Lee about fast tracking the purchasing of a new one."

I had an idea.

"I need your help," I said. "I need to get into Lee's computer."

"Absolutely not. There's no way we can pull that off."

"Yes, we can. I just left Lee's office. You need to rush in and tell him that the two of you need to talk to Gina right now. Tell him it will only take a minute."

"What reason do you suggest I give for needing to see Gina?"

"When you brought up the idea of creating and selling a calendar as a fundraising activity, how did Gina react?"

"She loved it. She wants—"

"Great. The calendar will require an initial outlay of money from the budget for printing services, right? That means you'll need to involve Lee. I want you to go to his office, and ask him to talk with you and Gina now. Tell him it will only take a few minutes."

"So, if I get Lee into Gina's office—and that's a big if—what will you do?"

"Hopefully, he won't shut off his computer for that brief time. Once you are both in Gina's room, I'll sneak into Lee's office. I need to find out where payments to the Relda Corporation are being sent."

"Do you have any *idea* of what will happen if someone sees you? Using the excuse of looking for a pencil in Wendy's desk is one thing. But sneaking into the business manager's office and searching on his computer is different. No one will believe you weren't snooping."

"If I get caught, I'll say I saw Lee's office was empty, and to save time, I wanted to see if he had next year's projected budget statistics for my magazine story. I'll take the blame. You won't get in trouble."

Declan remained silent. His arms were folded in front of his chest.

"This may help discover who killed Maureen and Wendy. Right now, you are the number one suspect."

Declan sighed. "I don't think this will work, but I'll give it a try."

We made our way into the building. I stood silently in the corner where neither Gina nor Lee could see me. I watched as Declan marched into Lee's office. A few moments later, the pair made their way into Gina's room. Declan stood in front of the doorway, blocking both Gina's and Lee's view of what was happening outside.

I scooted into Lee's office. His computer was on. But I didn't need it. On his desk was another bill from the Relda Corporation. This time, I paid attention to the address.

CHAPTER 62

The address for the Relda Corporation was a post office box. Back home, I let the dogs out in the back yard and then phoned Detective Fox and asked him to find out the name and address of the box owner. He said he'd get to it when Wolfe wasn't looking over his shoulder.

During the weekend, I continued my research. Relda was a corporation, so I searched the New York State corporation database, where I found the filing had been done by Lee Adler. Later, Detective Fox called me back and told me the Relda Corporation's post office box also belonged to Lee.

"It looks like he's defrauding the sanctuary," I said to Fox.

"Yes, but we still have no proof of murder."

Nothing much happened on the case until late Monday afternoon when Abby stopped by the house on her way home from work. She had the drawing her artist friend created of Lee Adler based on the photo I texted her. But this drawing gave him black hair and no glasses.

"I'm driving to the diner now to see Wilma. I want to see if she recognizes this drawing as the mystery man."

"Okay. But what are your plans for later? Jason has a bar association meeting, and Dad has evening hours at the veterinary hospital, so I thought we could have dinner together and discuss the case."

"Good idea. I have the Wolf Howl later tonight, but they're only serving dessert. Why don't I bring dinner home from the diner? How about spanakopita?"

"Sure, but it will never be as good as Aunt Melita's."

Spanakopita was a Greek dish made from spinach, cheese, and pastry. My aunt, from the Greek side of my family, made the best spanakopita I'd ever eaten.

"You're right," I chuckled. "But since I did not inherit cooking genes from my Dad's side of the family, the diner's spanakopita is the best I can do. Grandma will be home shortly too, so she'll be joining us."

My mother was currently out shopping for a sweater. She claimed my air-conditioning made her feel like an icicle.

"I'm going to run a few errands," Abby said. "I'll be back in an hour."

"Perfect. That should give me plenty of time to get to the diner, talk to Wilma, and drive back home. Wilma said she's working the evening shift this week. Let's hope she's there."

We both left the house and went our separate ways.

When I arrived at the diner, I was in luck. Wilma was busy waiting on tables and said she'd talk to me in a few minutes. I went to the counter and ordered our take-out. Finally, she arrived.

"I don't have a lot of time," Wilma said. "I thought the breakfast crowd was tough, but dinner hour is busier."

"This won't take long." I pulled out the drawing. "Do you recognize this person?"

She stared at the picture. "I do. It's the man who met that girl." Wilma looked up at me. "The girl in the photo you showed me last week—the murder victim."

BINGO!

I paid for my food and hurried home. Abby had returned and so had my mother. Both appeared comfortably situated in the living room. Abby was texting while my mother was reading a magazine.

"We've identified the mystery man," I said. "It's Lee Adler."

"That's great, but…"

"But what?"

"Lee may be cooking the books, and he may be the mystery man, but he's clear for the murder of Wendy, right?" Abby asked.

I frowned. "Unfortunately, yes. He has an alibi for the time she was killed. And I can't think who his accomplice could be."

I was wearing a new pair of strappy sandals today, and my feet hurt. "I'm going to put on my comfy slippers. Why don't you set the table? Then we can throw around some ideas as we eat. My thinking improves when I'm comfortable."

"And when you're eating." Abby grinned.

Abby headed toward the cabinets. I made my way upstairs and soon returned in my fuzzy bunny slippers.

Merlin spotted my slippers and immediately pounced on them.

"They're not real," I said, as I shook the cat off my feet. Brandy and Archie stared as if they never saw such odd behavior.

I poured three glasses of wine. Abby, my mother, and I sat down for dinner.

"So, who could be Lee's accomplice?" my daughter asked.

"Not Gina. She has an alibi. She and Lee were together at a luncheon in Manhattan. It would have to be Nick, Sam, or…"

"Declan." Abby completed the thought, but quickly added, "It can't be him."

"I agree." I paused. "I think."

"Where do the suspects claim to be at the time of Wendy's murder?"

"According to Detective Fox, they were all at different parts of the sanctuary. So no one has a verifiable alibi."

"Now that we know money may be the motive, does that help

narrow down the suspects?" Abby asked.

I took a bite of my spanakopita, finished chewing, and said, "Nick and Sam both have financial problems. Nick has large child support payments, and Sam's family lost everything when the restaurant closed."

We sat silently.

"Something's not right," I finally said. "My instinct tells me neither is involved. Work is not only a job to Nick and Sam, it's a calling. They love the animals. I can't imagine either of them doing anything that would hurt the sanctuary."

"Declan too. He could make a lot more money working somewhere else, but he wanted to work with these rescue animals."

"I'll let the two of you work on it," my mother said as she rose from her chair. "I want to finish the magazine article I was reading.' She grinned. "I'm surprised a young person like you buys hard copies instead of reading online."

I hadn't been called a young person in a while.

"That's Matt's magazine," I said. "He prefers physical copies. He says he spends enough time on the computer."

"There's a fantastic article on a scientist who unearthed a body frozen in time. The body is still in good condition." My mother smiled. "For a dead man."

"Of course. Decomposition stops when…" I paused.

Frozen in time.

"That's it." I jumped up from my chair.

"What's it?"

"Lee doesn't have an alibi for Wendy's death. The time of death is wrong."

"What do you mean?" Abby appeared puzzled.

"Decomposition stops when a body is frozen. If a body is refrigerated, the body still decomposes, but the decomposition slows down at a tremendous rate. It's often difficult to figure out the time of death. When Nick and I went into the food storage unit the other day, we found Wendy's necklace. He said she never had reason to go into that building."

I paused. "I believe she was murdered earlier in the day. And her body put in the refrigerated section to slow down decomposition."

"Making the time of death incorrect," Abby added.

"If Wendy was killed earlier, Lee could be the murderer."

CHAPTER 63

"What are you going to do?" Abby asked.

"I'm phoning Detective Fox. This may be circumstantial, but it's incriminating."

"I mean what are you doing about tonight's fund raiser?" A worrisome frown spread across Abby's forehead.

"The Wolf Howl? I'm attending."

"You're not confronting Lee there, are you?"

"If he's there, I'll avoid him. But I don't think he's coming. He's the business manager. He has nothing to do with the animals. According to the sanctuary's website, the nocturnal tour will be led by had animal keeper Nick Lamonica."

"Are you sure it's safe? Do you want me to come with you?"

"I'm attending on a special invite from Gina Garone. I can't bring another person. It will be fine." I grabbed my phone and punched in the phone number for Detective Fox. It went straight to voice mail, so I left the following message.

"Lee's been defrauding the sanctuary, and I think Wendy's body was refrigerated, which will change the time of death. I believe Lee murdered Maureen and Wendy. Please call as soon as you get this."

Later that evening, I drove to the sanctuary for the Wolf Howl.

As I made my way from my car to the path, I could feel the perspiration on my forehead, despite the cool breeze. I was getting closer to the truth, and it made me apprehensive.

I trudged up to the administration building. There was no lighting, but the full moon illuminated my way.

"We have lighting on the patio outside the administration building where we'll have dessert later," Nick explained once I joined him and the other guests. "We also have lighting in the habitats, but we only put it on after dark if there is an emergency, such as an animal needing medical assistance. Everyone needs to be on the lookout for our night creatures."

There were thirty people in attendance tonight plus Nick, Gina, and me. I relaxed a bit since Lee was not here.

"Let's get started on our tour of the nocturnal animals?" Gina said. "Nick will lead, and I will take up the rear. Everyone else should be in-between."

The sanctuary was different at night—full of shadows and strange sounds. The branch of a nearby dead tree resembled a snake ready to strike. A shiver spread up my spine.

As we trekked further into the sanctuary, the odor of rich earth filled the air. I could hear the howling of the wolves in the distance. We passed a leopard that Nick explained had once been someone's pet. We spotted several night creatures, including a fox, coyotes, and two owl monkeys. As we neared the wolves, the howling became louder. It was awesome.

Once the tour finished, we headed to the patio behind the administration building for refreshments. The howl of the wolves could still be heard in the distance. I grabbed a cup of coffee and was about to select a dessert when Gina approached. Her face was grim.

"Do you have all the information now for your story?"

"Yes." I nodded. "I'll be writing it up this week, so this is probably the last you'll see of me."

"I hope you portray the sanctuary in a good light."

"My focus is on the good work you do, including background on the horrific lives of these animals before they came here. Readers should be sympathetic."

I bit my lip. I hadn't lied—that would be the gist of my story. Although I didn't know if the murders would be solved by my deadline, I expected to verify the money scam shortly. If financial fraud was occurring, I would need to include that. I didn't want to hurt the sanctuary, but the public, especially the donors, had a right to know how the money had been spent.

I felt confident that once Gina and Carolyn found out about the scandal, they would implement safeguards to prevent it from happening again. I would make sure my story included any positive actions on their part. But all this had to be completed by my deadline.

I hoped the scandal wouldn't destroy this place. As much as I loved my job and believed in telling the truth, there were times like this when I hated what I had to do.

I was jostled out of my thoughts when a middle-aged woman, who had been on the tour with us, approached Gina. If she had been born a dog, she would have been a greyhound. The physical characteristics were all there: long legs, sleek body, and a narrow pointed face.

"Excuse me," she said. "I wanted to verify our meeting tomorrow. It's at ten o'clock, right?"

"Yes, Maggie." Gina nodded.

When the woman departed, Gina said to me, "Maggie is currently a volunteer. Lee and I are interviewing her tomorrow to hire as Wendy's replacement."

"Both you and Lee are conducting interviews?"

"Yes. Lee and I will do it together. Unfortunately, I was the only one who interviewed Wendy and that turned into a problem."

"Problem? How so?"

"Wendy liked to help. Sometimes she would take on tasks she wasn't assigned. One time, Lee returned from a meeting and discovered Wendy had straightened up his desk." Gina shook her head. "Lee was furious, I never saw him lose his temper before this. He said he knew where everything was until she put things in other places."

I smiled, remembering when Abby rearranged supplies in Matt's veterinary hospital. Matt was not pleased. But it sounded as if Lee had overreacted. Was this when Wendy had uncovered the financial fraud?

Gina continued. "Lee also told me Wendy asked too many questions, and he was way too busy to answer them. Since the receptionist works for both of us, Lee should have a say in whomever we hire."

Gina left to mingle, and I stayed at the dessert table, trying to decide what sweet should accompany my coffee.

After scarfing down a devil food cupcake, I noticed most of the guests had left. I glanced at my watch and realized I should leave too.

Before departing, I grabbed my phone. It had been on silent mode during the nocturnal tour, but a check of my voicemail told me that Detective Fox had called. I shot off a text telling him I would be heading home from the sanctuary now and would phone him from the car in a few minutes.

Before I had a chance to turn off the silent mode, a young woman approached. She said she was a college student majoring in journalism. Gina told her I was a reporter, and she wanted to ask me a few questions about careers in this field. A few questions turned out to take close to forty minutes, but I enjoyed the conversation and hoped I helped her.

Once she left, I noticed that only a middle-aged couple remained, plus Nick and Gina who were huddled in conversation at the far end of the patio. Clouds now blocked the full moon, bathing the ground in darkness. Since the path to the parking lot wasn't paved, I'd need to be careful not to trip and fall on my way out.

The middle-aged couple began heading toward the exit. They had come equipped with a flashlight. Luckily for me, they seemed to be engaged in a leisurely stroll. I caught up with them by the time they reached the path.

"Fun evening, wasn't it?" I said.

The woman nodded. "I got chills from the howls. It was wonderful."

"I found it interesting when Nick told us how wolves howl back in response to calls from others in the pack, acknowledging the original message," the man added.

We chatted until we reached the parking area. Their car was nearby, so they said good-bye as I continued to the end of the lot. By the time they exited, I had arrived at my car and was about to unlock my door when I felt a hand on my shoulder.

Something sharp poked my back.

"Don't move," a voice said. The tone was menacing.

It was Lee Adler.

CHAPTER 64

"What do you want?" I heard the quake in my voice. "What did Wendy tell you?"

"Wendy? Nothing."

I felt another sharp jab. "This is a knife," Lee said. "I will kill you if you lie."

If I told the truth, he would probably still kill me.

He poked again. I could feel the blade rip through my clothes and scratch my skin.

"Wendy and I barely spoke."

"You're lying," he said. "I have Wendy's cell phone. I know she contacted you the day before she died."

I thought quickly. "That call was about returning my husband's veterinary book. She borrowed—"

"No, it wasn't. I was leaving my office when she phoned you. She didn't know it, but I overheard her saying she had something to show you."

He paused. "It was that notebook, wasn't it?"

Before I could respond, he continued, "The police never found the notebook. Do you have it?"

"Yes," I said. I figured he would keep me alive a little longer if he thought I could get the notebook for him.

"Where is it?"

"In my office at *Animal Advocate*."

The notebook was not in my office. It was in my home, but I couldn't put my family at risk. And the office was closed until the morning.

"We're going to drive to your office now," he said.

"We can't get in. I don't have a key." I lied.

"I'll figure a way. Your magazine operates on a shoestring. I doubt the alarm system is state of the art."

I didn't think the building had an alarm system at all.

There were two cars in the sanctuary parking lot in addition to mine. Gina and Nick were still here. I remembered the old beat-up Honda belonged to Nick and I assumed the Jaguar was Gina's car.

"Where is your car?" I asked Lee.

"Parked in a shopping center about a quarter of a mile down the road. I walked from there." He snickered. "I came though the bushes. This way I wouldn't be caught on the security camera at the front gate."

"Gina and Nick may come down the path at any second," I warned him.

"No, they won't. I overheard Gina telling Nick earlier this afternoon that once everyone left the reception, she wanted to go over a new marketing idea with him—one involving the animals. She was meeting with some donors about it tomorrow, so she wanted to hash it out with him tonight."

I knew my best chance at surviving was to stall.

"You're siphoning money to a phony company—the Relda Corporation," I accused him. "You ordered food that was never delivered. But that didn't matter because it wasn't needed."

"It wasn't only food. I ordered lumber, cages, offices supplies, and more items that didn't come, and we didn't need."

"Maureen caught on?"

"Yes. Gina never paid attention to the nuts and bolts of the operation, and Nick and the rest of the staff only cared about getting what they needed for their animals. But Maureen stuck her nose where it didn't belong. She wanted to see if we could get a better deal from other companies. To do that she needed to know what we were currently ordering and how much we were spending."

"She discovered you ordered way more than you needed. She also snooped around and noticed that several orders never arrived," I said, accusingly.

He nodded. "That about sums it up."

"And Wendy?"

"She was a natural born snoop. She saw some bills from the Relda Corporation and became suspicious. Now, stop talking. Unlock your car. You're driving. I'll be in the passenger seat with my knife ready to gut you should you try anything."

I had to make a run for it. But I had a knife in my back.

My tote bag was huge. Matt always joked and said I could use it as a weapon. So, I did.

I spun around and whacked Lee with the bag. I hopped into my car and slammed the door shut. But before I could turn on the ignition, Lee swung open the door, grabbed my arm, and yanked me out, throwing me to the ground.

"You're a dead woman," he said. His face was frozen into an icy mask of anger.

Before he could act, I heard sirens in the distance. They became louder as flashing lights appeared on the horizon. Two police cars and a Crown Victoria careened into the parking lot.

"This is the police," a voice yelled through a megaphone. "Move away from the car with your hands raised."

Lee did as told. Detective Fox hopped out of the Crown Victoria and dashed toward me.

"Are you okay?"

I nodded. "How did you know to come—"

"When I phoned you earlier, you texted saying you would

call me back in a few minutes. That was almost an hour ago. I phoned you again, but it went straight to voice mail.

"You called me?" I realized my phone was still on silent mode.

"Your text message also said you were leaving the sanctuary. I stopped by your house and you weren't home. At this time of night, if you left as planned, you should have arrived by then."

I was grateful for the college student whose questions delayed my departure by more than a half hour.

"I figured something was up," Fox said.

"Something certainly was."

I started to tell Detective Fox what I had discovered.

He held up his hand and smiled. "Lee Adler almost murdered you. We have more than enough for an arrest. Tomorrow morning, come down to the station. Right now, you need to go home and get some rest."

A familiar car sped into the parking lot. Matt and Abby hopped out and came running toward me.

"Detective Fox told us you might be in trouble." Matt hugged me. "I'm so glad you're okay." He wiped his brow. "But you have to stop playing Jessica Fletcher."

"We'll see." We both knew that wasn't happening.

"I'm driving you home in your car, so you can relax," he said. "Abby will drive my car."

I grinned. "Great idea."

EPILOGUE

Three Weeks Later

"Isn't Abby with you?" I asked Jason after he entered the house and greeted the dogs in my kitchen.

"She'll be here in about thirty minutes. It's her friend Julia's birthday, and they went to dinner. Julia's leaving on a business trip tomorrow, and since she will be driving to the airport before dawn, they made early restaurant reservations."

"Isn't Julia one of Abby's bridesmaids?" my mother asked. "They'll probably be talking about the wedding." She sighed. "I wish I was a fly in that room."

I grinned. My mother didn't like being left out of anything.

Jason immediately changed the subject. "Your friend Marcia may receive good news," he said to my mother. "My white-collar crimes unit uncovered hidden assets belonging to Austin Briggs. We may be able to get some financial restitution for his victims."

"Some?" my mother asked.

Jason shrugged. "Briggs scammed a lot of investors. We don't know if there's enough to fully reimburse everyone for their entire loss, but at least all the victims should get some portion back. He paused. "They're lucky. In most pyramid schemes, victims never recoup anything."

The doorbell rang.

"Are you expecting anyone?" Matt asked.

"Yes." I made my way to the door, swung it open, and Declan Carr stepped into the house. I had invited him to our gathering to celebrate the end of the ordeal he'd suffered as an innocent suspect in the murders of Maureen McDermott and Wendy Wu.

"It's such a beautiful night. Why don't we go out on the patio?" Matt suggested.

"Good idea." I nodded. "But we have to wait for Abby before we start talking about the murders and the sanctuary's financial scandal. I know she has questions."

At my mother's request, Matt made margaritas. We gathered outside, engaging in small talk until Abby finally arrived.

"Any feedback on your story?" Abby asked as she settled into a lounge chair. The latest issue of *Animal Advocate*, which included my article, had come out last week.

"So far, so good." Although I did write about the murders and financial scandal, I'd put a positive spin on how the sanctuary administration was overhauling their financial management, including the immediate new safeguards they were putting in place.

I chuckled. "That old saying 'bad publicity is still publicity' turns out to be true. People who never heard of the Happy Place Animal Sanctuary are now aware of the good work it does in rescuing animals. Some of these people have sent in big contributions."

"Plus, Gina's husband is matching donations until it reaches one hundred thousand," Declan added.

"It's nice to be rich." I grinned. "When I saw that construction had stopped on Frank Garone's condominium project, I thought the Garones were in financial trouble."

"That was a municipal permit holdup. Gina talked about it yesterday," Declan said.

"It's all been straightened out, and the construction is back underway."

Declan sipped his soda. "To get back to the future of the sanctuary, I think we're on the right path. The new business manager has impeccable credentials, and although Gina's focus will still be fundraising, there will now be a series of checks and balances."

I smiled. "I'm glad Carolyn, as chair of the board of directors, has agreed to monitor the budget, too. I also love that Nick Lamonica has been promoted."

"What?" Abby looked surprised. "Do you mean he's no longer head animal keeper?"

"He now has dual titles. He'll stay as head keeper, but he'll also be assistant budget director. He knows what the animals need. With Nick paying attention to the ordering of supplies, there should be no shenanigans. And the extra work comes with a small raise, which Nick can definitely use."

"I still have questions you didn't address in your article," Abby said. "I'd like to know exactly how Lee committed the two murders."

I had played down the murders. The story's focus was the animals.

I sipped my margarita. "Everything was timing. Maureen had confronted Lee about what she uncovered. He offered to explain and arranged to meet her Monday at seven-fifteen by the bear habitat—that's way before anyone would be in that area. Lee also knew Declan arrived at the sanctuary at seven. On the day of the murder, Lee got to the sanctuary at six-thirty."

"We checked what employees were present that morning, but we never asked what time they arrived," Abby said before I could finish what I intended to say.

I continued, "Lee went straight to the veterinary infirmary and took the etorphine."

"But how?" Abby asked. "He didn't have a key."

"Yes. He did. As business manager, he was the one responsible for ordering all locks and keys. He had his own key made for the infirmary and for the medicine cabinet, but no one knew."

I grabbed a potato chip before going on. "Anyway, after stealing the drugs, Lee headed for his rendezvous with Maureen. No one else was around. He injected her with the etorphine and dragged her body into the bear enclosure. As he exited, he pulled the switch to open the cave doors and release the bear."

"On his way back to the administration building, Lee spotted me rescuing the distressed deer," Declan added. "He used that to his advantage. He told the police that I was not at the veterinary infirmary as I usually would be."

"Unbelievable." Matt shook his head. "What about Wendy Wu?"

"Pretty much the same. Lee confessed to the police that Wendy discovered discrepancies and threatened to expose him. He begged her to meet with him so he could explain. They met at the diner, and he told her he had papers in his car she needed to see.

"Is that when he killed her?"

I nodded. "The diner had a small parking lot, so during busy times, many customers had to park nearby and walk. Lee parked down the block behind an abandoned warehouse that backed up on the woods." I paused as I watched my husband hand my mother her second margarita.

I continued. "Once there, Lee injected Wendy with the etorphine, stashed her body in his trunk, and drove to the food storage unit at the sanctuary. Later that day, he went to the luncheon with Gina, knowing the slowed decomposition caused by the refrigeration would give an inaccurate time of death."

"And he would have an alibi," Jason added.

"Right. I remember running into Gina and Lee when they returned from their luncheon. We had almost reached the administration building when Lee announced he left his phone in his car and headed back to get it. That's when he drove to the storage area and removed Wendy's body from the refrigerated area and put it outside, near the pond."

"Clever," Abby nodded. "But I don't understand why they checked for etorphine in the first place—with Maureen. That's not a standard drug to test for in an autopsy."

"This new medical examiner is really sharp," Jason said. "She asked for a list of all drugs kept on the premises."

For a moment I stared up at the sky and gazed at the banana shaped moon. I listened to the crickets while I pondered all that happened. Then Abby jolted me out of my thoughts.

"How's your editor doing?" she asked.

"Fine. You would never guess that only a few weeks ago Olivia was hospitalized and fighting for her life. We get our new assignments on Monday."

"Any idea what your major story will be?"

"Not sure. Olivia may assign me a piece on Alaskan wildlife since your father and I are taking a cruise there in another week and—"

"I'm going, too," my mother interrupted. "Kristy and Matt are taking me there for my seventy-fifth birthday."

I continued. "According to Clara, who hears everything in the office, Olivia is also considering a story on the new Arctic exhibit at the Harborside Zoo or a feature on the Underwater Sea Institute in Montauk. I might be writing on one of those topics too."

Abby grinned. "It's funny. So far, you've written articles in four issues of *Animal Advocate*. For each issue, you've been involved in a murder investigation."

Matt frowned. "Funny! I don't think that's funny at all. Let's not have a fifth murder."

After sipping my margarita, I grinned. "A fifth murder? C'mon. What are the odds?"

ABOUT THE AUTHOR

A mystery fan since she read her first Nancy Drew novel, Lois Schmitt combines a love of mysteries with a love of animals in her series featuring wildlife reporter Kristy Farrell, which includes *Monkey Business*; *Something Fishy*, 2nd Runner-Up for the Killer Nashville Claymore Award; *Playing Possum*, Silver Falchion Award Finalist; and new from Encircle Publications in September 2024, *Bearly Evident*.

Lois is a member of several wildlife conservation and humane organizations, as well as Mystery Writers of America and the Long Island Author's Guild. She worked for many years as a freelance writer and is the author of Smart Spending, a consumer education book for young adults. She previously served as media spokesperson for a local consumer affairs agency and a teacher at Nassau Community College on Long Island.

Lois lives in Massapequa, New York, with her family, which includes a 120-pound Bernese Mountain Dog. This dog bears a striking resemblance to Archie, a dog of many breeds, featured in her Kristy Farrell Mystery series. For the latest news, follow Lois Schmitt on Facebook and Instagram (@LoisSchmittMysteries), and visit her website, loisschmitt.com.

If you enjoyed this book,
please consider writing a review
and sharing it with other readers.

Many of our Authors are happy to participate in
Book Club and Reader Group discussions.
For more information, contact us at info@encirclepub.com.

Thank you,
Encircle Publications

For news about more exciting new fiction, join us at:

Facebook: www.facebook.com/encirclepub

Instagram: www.instagram.com/encirclepublications

Sign up for the Encircle Publications newsletter:
eepurl.com/cs8taP

Printed in the USA
CPSIA information can be obtained
at www.ICGtesting.com
JSHW020005250724
66942JS00001B/20